Collecting Candace

Susan M. Brooks

small dogs press

A Small Dogs Press book
Seal Beach, California

Collecting   Candace.   Copyright   ©   2005
by Susan M. Brooks. All rights reserved. No part of
this publication may be used or reproduced in any
manner whatsoever without written permission, except in the case of brief quotations embodied in crit-
ical articles and reviews. For further information,
please contact the publisher.

Published by Small Dogs Press,
P.O. Box 4127, Seal Beach, CA 90740.

www.smalldogspress.com
info@smalldogspress.com

Library of Congress
Cataloging-in-Publication Data
Brooks, Susan M.
  Collecting Candace / Susan M. Brooks

Library of Congress Control Number: 2004097559

ISBN 0972932933

To AAK

I hope you see me.
xoxo

Sue

Collecting
Candace

chapter one

He met Candace in Gainesville, Florida, in the Hi-n-Dri 24-Hour Liquor and Mart, at 4 a.m. It was thirty days deep into the worst heat wave that all of Northern Florida had seen in over a hundred years. It was his fourth consecutive night of insomnia. And that should tell it all.

She was drinking a beer straight out of the bottle. He needed a Jack Daniels, no ice. He noted their different levels of tolerance. Later, he'd remember that moment and wish he wasn't so fucking observant sometimes.

Her skirt was appropriately short; her tattoo, colorful and a little obscene. He pictured them laying her out and painting some grotesquely illegal act on her thigh, and he could see her walking up and down the aisles of the flea market on Sunday, flashing it like a badge of courage. He admired how her clothes fit her and he thought of the poor bastard who was stupid enough not to notice these things.

He didn't know if she had a husband, but he imagined that if she did, he would like very much at that moment to kill him. And that's how all the trouble started.

Being there, in the Hi-n-Dri, didn't help much. Hell, being in Gainesville didn't help much. Situated nearly seventy-five miles south of the Georgia

Collecting Candace

state line, and smack in the center between coasts, Gainesville was, like most of Florida, hot more than anything else. It wasn't as flat as the rest of the state; much of the surrounding landscape could be described, in places, as hilly. In certain parts of town you could forget you were in Florida. In some places, thickly wooded backyards buzzed with insects and old dogs napped in the sun and rooted into empty chips bags. There were plenty of trees and even when it was hot, it was green. But there were also flying bugs that grew as big as a baby's fist, and it wasn't all that uncommon for gators to show up in a backyard wandering around looking for snacks, most of the time hungry for squirrels, field mice, or—if they were lucky—a cat. Gators were reviled by residents, especially those with small children, and school kids frightened themselves with stories about finding the skeleton of a half-eaten baby back in the woods behind someone's trailer. Some of the older boys had even sworn that they'd seen the remains, which now were wrapped in an old dog blanket and buried in a friend's older brother's cellar.

The human population of Gainesville was made up of three factions: University of Florida students, who kept mostly to their own kind; residents who went to Gator games, owned pizzerias close to campus, or supported higher education through their tenure at the college or through a job at McDonald's; and, lastly, hardcore locals—residents who lived on the fringes and were only incidentally aware of the "school" on the other side of town, folks who visited places such as the Hi-N-Dri for fun.

In a place like the Hi-N-Dri 24-Hour Liquor and

Mart, the days took forever to pass, but the years took hardly any time at all. Talk was most often centered around three things—dogs, fly fishing, and the heat.

Inside the Hi-N-Dri, that morning at four o'clock, there wasn't much talk of any kind.

It used to be a bright cafe with yellow vinyl booths inside and small tables and colored awnings outside, welcoming tourists passing through with a warm Southern hello and a bad Chinese chicken salad, slaw on the side. Now it was a seedy dive; weeknights it was jammed with women with their husbands' best friends, and sometimes vice versa.

When the Hi-N-Dri 24-Hour Liquor and Mart moved in, there had been little to do in the way of conversion, other than to apply for a state liquor license. Once that was secured, a pool table was moved in, along with a couple of booths—blood-red leatherette from the restaurant wholesaler—and sheets of corrugated fiberglass were nailed over the places where there used to be windows. Though half the sign said MART in big red letters, the only things not sold in a shot glass were individual packets of Alka-Seltzer, dehydrated ramen noodles and some stale candy bars.

During the day the clientele was quiet and manageable, made up mostly of retirees who stopped in for a cold one. But at four in the morning, when sober citizens were home in bed, those who lay in decay at the bar consisted of career insomniacs, "ladies" steeped in gin, and men who dream of girls named Cindi—all suffering in simpatico and trying best as they could to escape the sweltering heat.

Collecting Candace

And, of course, there was Candace, who was neither devastated nor suicidal, only bored.

This crowd earned the Hi-N-Dri a reputation for quiet trouble. Although it had never seen a knife fight and nobody had ever been killed in the parking lot, it would be bad if a man were to hear that his wife had been spotted out there.

Now he wondered who was lying in bed right now, waiting for the bad news about Candace being out there at four a.m. to hit him.

He wiped the sweat from his brow and then from behind his ear and nodded at the barkeep for another round, this time indicating ice on the side. He smiled crookedly at Candace, who had plopped herself down beside him and carelessly kicked his shins as she wiggled into position on the rickety stool. She dumped a beauty magazine, a Bible, and car keys onto the bar and introduced herself. As oddly as she was dressed and as openly as she placed herself next to him, he could not have mistaken her for a hooker. Not in a million years—and not this far off the main drag. He nodded blithely once in her direction, figured that she was waiting on her old man, who was either parking the 4-by or taking a piss out back, and turned his attention back to the whiskey that had just been brought by the bartender.

The walls of the Hi-N-Dri were thin, and to kill time, he listened to cars speeding by on the interstate. On some nights, some stupid tourist with a wagon full of kids driving straight through to Orlando would come in looking for the john and a Coke machine, but they never stayed long enough to even pull the money out of their pockets. One look at outer Gainesville's shiftless, rootless denizens would tell anybody that the Howard Johnson's might as well be a million miles away. Poor kids would have to hold it a little while longer.

And if the regulars didn't scare them away, Tip, a mangy mutt with no back feet, surely would. He was a fearsome sight for those on their way to Disneyworld, what with two perfectly formed front legs and feet but absolutely none in back, just a couple of smooth, blunt stumps where his toes should have been. He'd been named by some wiseass not for the two stubs he was cursed with, but because he never went tip-toeing across the floor like other dogs do, their nails clicking over the floor when they walked. He just went Tip.

It was speculation around the Hi-N-Dri that Tip lost his back feet to a stray gator, and that was enough to put a bounty of free beer for a month on the skin of the first one that came rambling into the bar. The reward had sat uncollected for nearly three years, but there wasn't a man in there who didn't twitch with anticipation every time a dog or a kid or something else low to the ground came poking its head in through the back door.

Regulars had a soft spot for Tip; they fed him beef jerky and leftover bites of jelly donuts that they'd cleaned out of their cars, stuff like that, that a dog just loves to death. Most nights he'd wander up and down in front of the bar, licking up beer froth and getting stoned on Pabst. Weeknights, when business was slow, he'd get a few good licks in and then go lie down under the pool table. Saturday nights, usually, he'd crawl out back and throw up from all the Wild Turkey that spilled off the bar.

Ten minutes went by and Candace's date had not arrived, and he wondered if it was possible that she had come alone into such a hole. It was too late for a woman to be out alone; it was too hot for anyone to be out, period. The thermometer behind the bar was reaching for eight-five, and here it was, barely ten after four. Watching Candace and that dog, it seemed to him that lately it was hot everywhere he went. Even when the sun was on the other side of the world in fucking China, it was still hotter than hell in Gainesville, Florida, and maybe that's why he hadn't slept in so long.

There was no air conditioning, just a trembling metal fan perched up on top of the platform where the TV used to be before the tube went out. That had been nearly six months ago, but everyone at the bar still sat there and stared up in the corner like they were waiting for wrestling or something. It took nearly a full minute to swing just four or five inches, but it was all that was going on that morning.

He and Candace were sitting at the far end of the bar, where the breeze was all used up by the time it reached them. Candace didn't seem to mind much. She chatted and swung her barstool around and around, pivoting herself a full 360 degrees, feet dangling and all, and then back again, mindfully ignoring the customers who leered at her from under the single white bulb that hung over the pool table near the back.

Tip whined some from underneath Candace's barstool. No telling if it was the heat or what that he was on about, so the others paid him no mind.

They'd just say, "Hush, Tip," and look back up at the fan. Candace tossed him pieces of ice and he wrestled with them on the dirty floor and then he'd try and get up onto her lap to lick her fingers, but it hurt to stand on his back legs and he'd just cry some more.

Charlie Parker played on the jukebox. It was nice. It was better than sleeping, anyway.

He fell for her in almost no time at all. That was usually the way it happened when it was for real.

He spent the next part of the evening wanting her badly; and even thought about trying to kiss her when she was laughing at her joke about the dog with no legs, being reminded about it 'cause of Tip and all. But when he leaned in, she swung another one-eighty on her bar stool, and his cheek just brushed over her bare shoulder. It was good. Close enough.

An hour later, she had just gotten through with the parts that brought her to the Hi-n-Dri. Catholic school and catechism, alcoholic father, food stamps and three former husbands—Danny Ray, Bobby Lee, and Joe. Just Plain Joe. By her own account, she was twenty-six and a half.

As he spent more time sitting beside her, he came to watch her more closely and enjoy not just her overall beauty, but all the things that she was made up of.

Her hair looked brown, but she swore it was blonde, dishwater blonde ("but no darker," she was quick to point out), and it was long, stick-straight. It was cut in one length all the way around, except in front where she had messy, thick bangs that, when

Collecting Candace

laid flat on her face, reached almost down to her lower lashes. It was just too dark to tell about the color of her eyes, but they were big and round and when her bangs were pushed away and not falling in the way, they were right out there in the open where they kind of made him nervous. She looked right at him when she talked, or when he did, and every time their eyes locked together it was always he who would avert his gaze first. Even when she spoke of serious things, her eyes glinted like she was laughing inside.

The rest of Candace was probably pretty standard through anybody else's eyes, though all put together there was something that seized his imagination almost from the start, when she kicked him in the shin and it hurt more than he let on. Her nose was a little wide in the bridge, her upper lip was noticeably thinner than her bottom, and her neck was long and slender and he liked to see her wrap her hair up top of her head so that he could see the stray wisps of hair there in the back that curled around her earlobes.

One thing he noticed right away and was glad for, was that she didn't have that fucking awful habit of chewing on her hair. God, how he hated girls who chewed on their hair. He told her this and then he asked her if she knew the story about the fifteen-year-old girl who up and died one day in school. They pumped her stomach and found a hairball; big as a grapefruit, inside of her, and Candace's eyes grew wide and all she could say was, "Well, there you go," as if to imply well, hell, what did she expect would happen, anyway?

He winked at her and smiled and she laughed loudly and said he was full of it but he swore, no, it was God's honest truth. Happened up in Tallahassee, was on the news some time last year.

Whatever little she did not tell him about herself, that Bible—and the magazine—on the bar beside her keys did. The Bible because the spine was not cracked, though at least a dozen scraps of paper poked out from between the pages here and there marking some passage or prayer or something. The magazine because from it she read her horoscope for the month of September. She was relieved to read that the stars were in her favor, that her love planet was on the rise—or some such shit—and that she could expect to come into money soon. This in particular pleased her, and she scanned the bar with narrowed eyes, maybe expecting to see a five-dollar bill wadded up underneath one of the stools. But there wasn't any there.

He looked at that Bible and asked her if she'd read any good books lately and she just sighed and said no and he let it slide.

Candace loved to talk. Her stories were strung out and hardly ever seemed to end anywhere. He liked that. He thought it was cute that she couldn't tell a story to save her goddamned soul. An older woman at the other end of the bar, sitting just below the fan, lit a clove cigarette, and the smell of it sparked Candace's imagination.

She took a deep breath of the rank aroma and smiled. "That's nice, like perfume. Reminds me of things." She didn't say what.

"Did you know..." She straightened in her seat

and leaned forward again. "...that the sense of smell is your strongest sense? Did you know that?"

He didn't.

"Even stronger than your eyes, can you believe it? That's a true fact."

She breathed in the heavy spice and shut her eyes. "Sometimes I smell something, and it reminds me of people, and things. It's nice, it's like being there," Her grin faded. "My house always smelled like milk, you know? Cereal milk." She crinkled her nose in disgust, and goddamned if he couldn't smell it too. "Gets in the bowls, the smell, I mean. You can never wash it out. Once it's in, it's set for life." He believed her.

She'd lived in that house four times, once when she was born there and all during her growing up, and again after each of her husbands. That would make four all together, including the stretch that had begun in April of this same year.

She talked about leaving and said she didn't know how much longer she could live with that smell. Had considered it often, but decided to stay. She was sure that her father, once dead, would leave her the house.

He reminded her that she'd have to throw the cereal bowls away first thing, and she giggled.

Like sickly relations and the smell of cereal milk, bad news was something that Candace had lots of to share, but the sight of her thighs disappearing into the short white skirt helped hold his attention as she reenacted the cataclysmic events that had shaped her life. The scent of her hair, even in the stale, smoke-filled lounge, drew him in. It smelled like the sheets after making love.

In the darkness, she looked barely old enough to drink, but she crouched over her beer with the self-protective posture of an experienced woman. Once, she threw her hands over her head and stretched and it was the first time in his life that he could smell his fear. It burned his eyes and made his mouth go dry.

He thought her to be one hell of a mystery, despite how she gave up most everything about herself freely—names of people and things that had happened to her, good or bad, she happily shared. He knew where she had been born (West Texas) and why she didn't like to wear panties underneath her jeans (too uncomfortable). The image he was left with was hardly a sketch like other women give

I like red roses and men who aren't afraid of success

but rather a detailed roadmap to her soul. Still, most things she told him were just things still. And if he had to point the way there, from here, he would have been unable to do it. This, he decided, was not due to any deception on her part but a dulling of vision on his.

The women he had been with before had clouded his judgment. When he looked at Candace and tried to see love, all he could really see was the tiny bedroom closet back at the house. How it always looked half empty, his shirts pushed to the right and crushed to make room for the loads of things crammed into the rear of whomever's hatchback had last crowded his driveway. He learned eventually that E for effort means shit. And no matter how he combed his hair or wore the collar of his jacket, he was always

Collecting Candace

mistaken for Him. The one who drank, the one who slapped her, the one who slept around, the one she couldn't forgive.

He wanted to say fuck it and draw Candace near, wrap his arms around her and bury his face in her neck. He wanted to cry on her shoulder and hand himself over just once without wondering how bad it would be when the first blow came, but he needed some clues before going and spilling it all on this strange, beautiful girl. Was someone waiting up for her? If he excused himself to the bathroom, would she be gone when he returned? Should he ask her to stay, or should he just stiff her with the check and go home to sleep it off?

He toed the line and leaned into the bar, wanting desperately to marry her and watch her grow old, but afraid that one night as he lay sleeping beside her she would reach over and strangle the life out of him.

His latest had been an insomniac like himself. She would rest on her elbow in the darkness and trace her fingertips over his face, as if she were trying to feel his goodness, as if it were powerful stuff that would respond to her simple touch. But her searches were half-hearted and she was easily diverted by her suspicions, deficiencies she thought she saw the beginnings of in the lines around his eyes. Doubt, fear, weakness. Women were so stupid. What had been sublimated since adolescence in a man's soul they naively expected to see smeared across his face as he slept.

Candace's order for a Coke, no ice, brought him back to the Hi-N-Dri 24-Hour Liquor and Mart, back to Candace, but it was in the middle of her telling of The Blessed Virgin Mary story that he felt the rope tightening.

Candace said She was plastic and almost perfect, except for that line that ran up both Her sides and over the top of Her head like a scar. From the mold. The statuette was her mother's. She'd told Candace that the Blessed Virgin Mary would protect her always and keep her faith alive. Candace's mother carried it in her bag for years, tucked safely into the pouch on the side for makeup and spare change.

She probably would have carried it forever if she hadn't lost it first. It toppled out her purse when she was stuffing the last of her suitcases into the trunk. She didn't even notice as it fell to the ground and bounced underneath the car. Candace was only nine, but she remembered wondering if that was when her mother lost her faith. The woman backed out the drive, waving a mascara-stained handkerchief out the window where it was cracked just a little. She narrowly missed the plastic statuette that lay in the driveway, and then she pulled away.

Candace liked to think that it was divine intervention, that she was meant to carry the piece in faith. Kind of like a rite of passage. Still, it didn't change the fact that She was left by accident.

Candace picked the tiny holy figure out of a grease spot in the drive and flinched a little when she felt her father's day-old whiskers brush against her cheek. He touched the plastic piece and looked down the long driveway.

"She can't help you now, Candy."

Candace kept the statue with her always. When

she was with Bobby Lee, her second, it sat by the kitchen sink, teetered on the window sill, "...so's I could look at Her when I did my chores sometime."

One day, She just fell in. Parts of Her were shredded up and got jammed in the garbage disposal. The landlord got mad and jacked up their rent by $20 and then Bobby Lee got mad and left Candace. Before he went, he told her that Catholic girls were no goddamned good, but she knew it wasn't about the rent or the day spent fighting over it. It was about faith and being left behind. It was about unconditional love and why did she need it so bad like she did anyway. And then he left.

Back in the Hi-n-Dri, he ordered a soda water and watched her trace over the front of her blouse, trying to make the sign of the cross. She couldn't remember which side to touch first, or if it even mattered.

She told him how she still had night sweats about the rescued Virgin Mary that was now glued to the dashboard of her Maverick. How every time she leaned into a right turn she saw the mangled plastic bits that should have been her hands. And she remembered the sound of Bob Lee's engine turning over, right before he pulled out of the gravel drive, just like the gnawing, mashing teeth of the In-Sink-Erator that almost ate Her up.

Candace was full of surprises. Like looking for bugs under the big rocks in the backyard where he grew up, pushing them aside and then finding an old nickel instead.

She asked him what he thought of heaven and he had to admit that he didn't know. She was glad. She delighted in telling him what she knew.

"Heaven's big as all outdoors," she whispered, as if revealing a well-guarded secret. "Room for everyone. For you, for me."

But was there room for Danny Ray and Bobby Lee and Joe was what he wanted to know.

She giggled at having almost been tricked and then nodded her head. 'Specially for Joe.

He felt a pang of jealousy and tried to let it go, but it stuck for a good minute or two.

He smoothed his hair back with the palm of his hand and stared at his reflection in the big mirror over the bar. He was thinking about purity. About innocence. How if he'd ever met anyone who should have it, it was her.

While they were talking, the door to the storeroom opened and a shaft of white light sprang up out of nothing and shot across the floor, straight for Candace. It hit the back of her head and lit her all up from behind. He wondered if it was all that talk about Catholics that was getting him worked up.

He watched her, with that halo round her head and all, thinking about how she looked so holy. And she just kept talking.

She told him secrets, things about herself, things about her husbands, that he was embarrassed to know. Candace probably talked to everyone like that. The clerk at the market. The bank teller. Instant intimacy. But none everlasting.

It was written all over her face. Emotional surrender, the murmured post-coital offerings that seemed to turn her bed into a confessional. He tried to imagine her as a virgin and kicked himself for not being there then. He wondered where the first scar had landed, how long it had been there, and how the fuck was he going to get rid of it anyway?

He didn't want to believe that her story had been heard before, but the unaffected, intimate manner in which she talked told him the path to Candace's heart was probably as worn as the fucking truck lane on I-75. Sharing a cigarette on the back porch, or telling jokes from behind the funnies on Sunday morning, she'd already let slip the little bits of information that shaped her soul.

Those endearing bad habits, idiosyncrasies, things that only a lover could appreciate, had been trodden over and abandoned by men who just happened to be in the right place at the right time. With each telling of a childhood memory or a private joke, the essence of her was spread more thinly. Every time she lost her temper or lay vulnerable in a lover's arms, she let go more of the only stuff that could catch a man and keep him forever.

All he knew so far was stuff: that she loved fountain drinks and hated the smell of cereal milk. He wondered in what order the rest would come and how long it would take.

It was an old story. By the time any of the others had reached his door, they'd been divvied up between so many others that they couldn't help but be diluted.

With them, it didn't matter. They could keep all that shit for all he cared. But with Candace, he was willing to knock on every door in the state of Florida, if that was the only way to get it back.

It was a bad situation. It needed fixing.

He had decided all of this before she even knew that she was his.

Bobby Lee was the worst, the one who took the most with him when he left, and that seemed the logical place to start. As they pulled out the gravel drive of the Hi-n-Dri 24-hour Liquor and Mart, the sun was still more than an hour away but it might as well have been straight up in the sky. The temperature outside the car must have been ninety, even hotter inside. There were lots of places to go on a morning such as this, lots of ways to try and cool off, but a road trip seemed like a good idea. Seemed like the best idea yet.

Later, when he was groping through the darkness of a strange man's apartment, feeling the sharp corners of an unfamiliar floor plan with his wet hands slippery on the Louisville Slugger, he wondered if the stupid sonofabitch even remembered The Blessed Virgin Mary incident; and, if he'd known it was a test of faith, would he still have left her anyway? Questions like these disappeared when the polished wood made contact with Bob Lee's skull, and in an instant, it was over and didn't matter anymore what he might have done.

She wanted to stop in the kitchen afterward to feed the dog 'cause she didn't know how long before it would be fed proper. The house was closed up tight, it was stuffy and dark, and it took him nearly twenty minutes to coax the poor dumb beast out from behind the couch while she opened the can of food and left fresh water. Her dark silhouette moved gracefully through the cramped kitchenette. She found her way easily, even with no light. He leaned back against the counter and folded his arms and watched her, thinking how right this was. He was feeling proud.

When she opened the fridge to get a soft drink, the kitchen was flooded with that flat, white light from inside, and he saw that some of the blood had smeared across her white skirt. The sight of it jarred him and he spun around to splash cold water on his forehead. His scalp tightened, his chest too, and it was hard to breathe. He shut the water off and led her out the back door, guiding her gently with his palm in the small of her back, careful not to touch her skirt, and all he could think of was that it was all still a fucking shame.

He didn't speak on the way back. He watched the sun come up over the Florida dust and stared at the mutilated Mother of God, wondering if Candace would make love to him when they got home.

He wanted to know how she was and if everything was still okay but he was afraid to ask. So instead, he stuck his face out the open car window and felt the hot wind on his face. Something in the car didn't smell right, it was damp and musty, smelled rotten. He panicked for a moment, felt something catch in his throat and tried to cough it up. He watched as Candace's red fingertips pushed away some stray blond hairs from around her face, and without giving it too much thought he settled into the leatherette seat and reminded himself it was fate that brought them together, and faith that would hold them tight.

He shook off the negative thoughts, knowing it would be different now. With each swing of his

bat, he returned to her the self-deprecating obser-
vations and tender remembrances of doomed cou-
plings that once lay in trust deep in her memory,
the things she had shared so eagerly in the name of
love. With each sharp crack that pealed through that
darkened house, they began their descent back into
her soul and took their place alongside the tortured
anecdotes of adolescence, and the things that you
couldn't understand about her unless you were still
in the thick of falling in love.

Five minutes onto the interstate, he finally, after
four nights of sleeplessness, nodded off, his head
pressed against the window. He heard the crack of
the bat in his dreams, like an aging high school ath-
lete reliving his glory days, and woke up sweating,
but fell again into sleep almost instantly. Whatever
remorse might have crept to the surface in any less
a man was easily extinguished by the very clean
conviction that he was right. That his actions were
just. It was the same pure logic that was adopted by
defense attorneys and their clients, men who pasted
local headlines to the kitchen wall. But he knew better. He could see through all that, and he knew he'd
be able to sleep again.

A while later they stopped and had take-out
breakfast in the car.

It was just after seven when they got to his house,
just in time to feed the cats, who'd gone without
food since the day before. A bunch of them ran toward the car as it swung into the drive, and Candace
narrowly missed the small one, the orphaned tabby.
He closed the house up tight, drew the blinds and
curtains and stayed with her under cover of dark-

ness. Then he changed the sheets for her, and she fell asleep instantly. While she lay there, her stained skirt still clinging to her hopelessly curved hips, he wondered what it does to a man to have your little girl mistaken for a woman in the eyes of other men. He pushed her hem up with the toe of his snakeskin boot and admired again the tattoo on her thigh. With a ballpoint, he tried to copy the design on his arm, but the way she tossed in bed made it hard to get a clear view, and all he could manage was a crude likeness.

He spent the next hour wandering around the house in the dark, taking care to be quiet and not play the radio too loud. And hoping for Candace to wake up, which she did not do. He sat and watched her most of the time, hoping that there'd be a sign, from Jesus or Mary, whoever took care of such things for Catholic girls. But Candace slept soundly. She gave nothing away, and it was just like watching the dead.

There was plenty of time to contemplate what he'd done; to regret it, too, maybe – but no time to take it back. Not that he would have. It was just another thought that came to him in those long, silent hours spent watching the woman he loved.

The temptation to look into his own eyes dogged him, but he was careful not to catch sight of his reflection in the small mirror that hung by the front door. He was curious. He'd heard that crimes like murder change a man forever, and though he didn't feel like he'd crossed any kind of threshold, he knew it was more than likely that nothing would ever be the same again.

After a while he turned on the TV, watching it with no sound so he could hear the sirens coming up the road. None came though. A couple of cars going by was all he heard, but nobody slowed as they passed his house, just like always.

He should have crashed alongside of her but was still feeling the buzz of the kill and was not worried that his insomnia was back.

He watched her some more and was kept company by the stories she'd told him earlier in the evening.

Please let it be me.

She slept peacefully and was easy to watch, even in the dead blue light of the TV. It soaked her skin from head to toe and then spread out all over the sheets like she was lying in a pool of electric blood. The random, staccato flashes that came from the screen alternately lit up and then doused all life around him. One minute she'd be a shaded silhouette on his bed, and the next something on the TV would spark up and it would flood the room in blue-tone again, getting in her hair and in his eyes.

When she was sleeping, as she was, no clear, concrete reason for loving her as he did could come to mind. When she was awake and looking straight at him, all he knew was that he wanted her. But once admitting to that, he would have to go even farther and acknowledge that he must have her.

He remembered wanting to be a cowboy once, and wondered for a minute what had happened to that dream and who might have taken it with them mistakenly, along with her makeup kit and favorite pillow. But cowboys and Indians, shit like that, didn't matter anymore if Candace would stay. He knew it was probably stupid to think in such simple terms, but sacrifice and surrender was all he knew love to be, and damned if he was going to get stuck on a technicality now that he'd come this close to heaven.

There was the pain she spoke of earlier, in the Hi-N-Dri, and he imagined that the rest of the night would just bring more of the same. He wondered could she be dreaming the same things he was thinking, or was that too much to ask for?

He thought of all that she had told him about the other one. He hadn't been to Georgia for some time, but he knew that he would be up for the trip. But planning that far ahead could be dangerous. She might wake up

Who the fuck are you?

full of regret and pretending not to know what they done and seen. Pointing that finger at him, beyond him and into that dark apartment

Officer I swear I had no previous knowledge of what this maniac was going to do.

But hadn't she told him that she loved a good long drive? And hadn't they had a good time just today, driving and talking and getting breakfast sandwiches to go?

Finally, around ten, he began to feel the weight of her companionship. He switched off the TV and then kicked off his boots and lay beside her in his twin-sized bed, taking care not to smudge his tattoo on the clean sheets. He knew that things would be different now; mostly he liked to think that he'd made them so. He fell asleep wondering when they would make love, anticipating the smell of her hair, and how it would feel falling down on his face from above.

Around noon, sleep came for the second time since he'd met her. He was anxious to finish this day and start the next, ready to pack up the car and head out for Decatur, where that bastard Danny Ray had gone back home after the divorce.

He was even more determined to rid their lives of all that complicated shit.

chapter two

He awoke after dark, instinctively throwing on yesterday's dirty clothes and setting about organizing the gear he kept stashed in a knapsack way in the back of the front closet. Even this late, with the sun gone for hours, he could still feel the heat swelling up around his head. Drops of perspiration clung to his mop of brown hair and slid down his back as he tried to navigate the darkened house. He moved clumsily, banged the bed twice with his knee, and winced at the thought of awaking Candace too soon.

There wasn't much space to stay out of her way; the kitchen, the bathroom, and the living room were the only places where he could sit and pass the time. There was a second bedroom, but no bed. It had been carted off by the last one's new boyfriend, oh, some time ago. There was no reason to go in there now, maybe to get a clean shirt out of the closet every now and again. The bureau was gone too, another claimant having already dug her nails into it.

There was no standing in the kitchen at all. Dirty dishes were piled everywhere and there wasn't even a table anymore. Nobody'd stolen it off of him, it had been broken up in a fight some time last year when one of the legs was pulled off in a moment of anger and wielded by an irate woman.

Collecting Candace

It could have been a nice house at one time. The paper was peeling and it sorely needed a fresh coat of paint, but such improvements were best left to young couples with babies and others as enthusiastically inclined. He just left it the way it was and was contented enough.

He stood awkwardly in the bedroom, looking down at her sleeping body.

She had moved little during the day and she was all rumpled in the clean white sheets. Her skirt was smudged with the dark stains from the day before. With no light, it was hard to tell what those stains were, but he knew. He had been there, he'd seen the red streaks on her when they were fresh, had watched her curl up in bed and fall asleep with the markings of a dead man staining her soft white flesh.

It seemed to bother her now about as much as it did then.

He stood over her for a moment, watching her chest rise and fall rhythmically with each breath. His tattoo was wet with perspiration and most of it had smeared off while he slept. But the lines of hers were still clear and distinct against her leg.

Standing above her, like he was, he knew that he wasn't seeing anything that hadn't been seen before. The others, they'd rolled over to see her at four in the morning, at midnight, and dawn, and dusk too. They'd seen the angle of her face just so, and probably got all excited when they'd seen how her body started to light up all over when the sun began to rise and the streak of warm light inched its way up those legs.

He suddenly remembered that she was a Catholic and wondered what the hell kind of dreams a Catholic girl has. He grinned to himself. Wild, he thought. Stained-glass Technicolor. He once knew a Catholic girl who had fantasies of making it with a priest. She said it was every Catholic girl's dream, and even made him come to bed one night wearing a white collar, just like the padres do. It was kinky, and he liked it, but when he tried talking about it once, without the shroud of night, she hushed him and made him promise never to mention it again. Said it was just bedroom talk, that's all. Like some Mexican girls holler Ave Maria when they're in the middle of their moment.

He wondered whether, if he'd been Catholic, too, he could forgive the others. That was the thing about never having faith. You ever needed absolution and the quality of your mercy had never been tested.

He sat Indian-style on the floor at the foot of the bed and opened the knapsack. Aside from the gun, which was cocooned separately in a leather pouch, there was a small hand towel that reeked with old dried sweat. He found the wrappers of two granola bars and a hundred or so spent shells. They jingled in the plastic sandwich bag as he lifted them out, but he palmed them with his other hand and set them aside so's they wouldn't disturb her sleep.

The last time he'd used the gun was at the range. It wasn't a real range, just an isolated field where guys would come on the weekends and shoot at pyramids of empty Bud cans and an occasional squirrel.

I'm no sportsman, but I sure can kill a can of Bud.

Collecting Candace

Just the gun and one bullet would have done the job, but that seemed such a meager plan that he began scouting the small house for items that might come in handy. First he found a length of rope. He held it in his fingertips and stretched it across his chest. It barely went the whole length, so he unplugged the TV and threw in the six-foot extension cord as well. Tape was next. An almost-empty roll of duct tape and a fresh roll of electrical tape. He tossed them both into the growing arsenal on the living room floor and stood over it, hands on his hips as his body pivoted and his eyes scanned the room for other useful weaponry.

The temperature inside the cluttered house was still rising, but not so's he'd notice.

A change of clothes, provisions that would get them through a couple of days at least, and some bottled water. He began pacing from room to room, plotting the perfect crime and digging up all the necessary accoutrements. He dug an old Bowie knife with a dull blade out of his underwear drawer and tossed it onto the heap. Hefty bags came next.

His genius for murder was of little comfort when perched so precariously on the edge of total madness.

Chloroform, a hypo, a silencer... he didn't know where to get these things, but he was sure that he needed them. He began to map out a plan in his head, how he would approach the man, what he would say. He scribbled some unintelligible notes on a scrap of paper.

A mask! Stockings!

Candace wasn't wearing pantyhose, and he was

disappointed.

His pile of armaments had grown from a few ne-
cessities into an unmanageable and paranoid pile of
junk. He circled it once, surveying the array of items
he'd collected for his outing with Candace. With the
toe of his boot he gingerly picked at the belongings
stacked there, pushing aside clean underwear and
separating the length of rope from the insulated
cord. He dug his toe in deeper and began kicking
out stray bullets that had been splashed all over the
floor.

He wondered where all this fight had come from,
and what was so special about that silly bitch anyway. He sat on the edge of his bed and wanted to cry,
but just sighed when Candace stretched her leg out
and brushed her bare shin up against his thigh. Even
clad in the thick blue jeans, his skin prickled when
she came near.

He racked his brain for all the things his father
had taught him. Guy stuff. Stuff about sports and
women.

His eyes drifted toward the corner of the living
room where the bloodied baseball bat still leaned
against the wall as he slid back into place on the
floor.

How to hit a home run.

If it were not for the scent of Candace, the constant reminder of his quest, he might have gotten
into his truck and just driven away. Maybe up north,
maybe to see his mother. But the sound of Candace's
nearly nude body rustling in the sheets behind him,
just there, over his left shoulder, wouldn't let him
be. It stirred him some, just enough to push him fur-

Collecting Candace

ther, a little bit at a time.

Thankfully, the sweltering heat had quelled most of the desire that he had suffered from the night before.

With a sigh, he leaned over and picked a single bullet from underneath the rubble. Tucking it into his jeans pocket, he pushed aside the other junk and began rummaging through the knapsack for the canister of cleaning fluid and some cotton patches, laying them side by side on the rug before him. His fingers reached across the floor and he cupped his hands around the smooth leather pouch that held his Luger.

By nine, he had more than ably prepared himself for the execution of his plan. His bag had been placed neatly against the wall by the front door. A fresh change of clothes was folded and resting on the back of the sofa. He had even managed to dig up some old jeans and a T-shirt for her to wear. But how he loved the way she looked in those clothes she was wearing. That short white skirt and how it didn't give even an inch around her smooth buttocks and tight thighs. He saw the red stains and how they had set in the fabric, and at that moment that washed-out shade of pink made all the difference in the world. His delight was almost pornographic.

He set out extra cat food, not knowing for sure how long it'd be before he came home again.

By ten o'clock, he'd had enough time to change his mind and then back again at least four times. What had happened yesterday, at Bobby Lee's, that was a crime of passion if ever he'd seen one. But tonight, his intent with regards to Candace's ex-husband was written all over his face. It cluttered the house and threatened to suffocate him if she didn't wake up soon and get him the hell out of there.

He had even made it out the front door once, but only by a couple of steps before he came to his senses and went back inside. He didn't want to do it again, but the thought of losing himself inside of her was almost more than he could bear.

He enjoyed wanting her. Enjoyed the anticipation damned near as much as he thought he'd enjoy the act. But it wasn't the thought of fucking her that had driven him this far. It wasn't sex he was killing for. Sex with Candace was just a symptom of the overall condition. You didn't have to be her lover to know that.

He stood above her and looked down and he knew that she was right. Timing is everything. If she had come to him last night, it would have been more like a gratitude thing.

It was nearly eleven-thirty, and Candace had still not awoken. She had had only one beer and a coupla Coca-Colas the night before, so it must've been something other than a hangover that made her want to hold onto unconsciousness.

Her sleep in the last half-hour or so had been fitful, the kind of slumber that was almost done with. He'd watched her eyes flutter like they were going to open. He'd get all anxious about her getting up and sitting with him and he even thought about making her something to eat, but then her eyelids would quiet down and lie still again. He'd breathe a sigh of relief and settle back down into the overstuffed chair to wait some more.

Collecting Candace

Finally, just after midnight, her eyes did open. They fixed on his immediately, like she'd been watching him through the skin of her eyelids the whole time.

How in the hell do you do that?

The edge of the sheet was just covering her mouth, but he could tell from the way her eyes were slightly squinted that she was smiling at him.

"I had this dream...." Her voice was low and throaty, sexy. "It was awful...."

He leaned forward to reach for her, but when her hand slid out from underneath the sheet, he could see dried blood underneath her long fingernails. He leaned back in the chair and set his boots on the edge of the bed. She wiped the corner of her mouth with the back of her hand and sat up. Her long legs kicked off the rest of the sheets, and she tried to swing them over the edge of the bed, but her skirt was too tight.

He thought he'd nearly die when she lay back and slid the skirt down over her hips, exposing a pair of French-cut panties with the word "Sunday" embroidered in blue up near the elastic waistband. Even from where he sat, he could see the little blond hairs covering that soft patch of skin on her belly, just below her navel. He imagined how it would feel against his cheek, how he could press his face against her body like he was listening for the sound of the sea. He imagined how those little hairs would sway back and forth over his skin like the fucking wheatfields of Nebraska.

"...just awful...."

He dragged his gaze up her body to lock his eyes

onto hers. He was envious of how she could make them look so soft and innocent on a morning such as this.

Upon Candace's awakening, his plans for the day had been set in motion. He had embarked on a course that, even in only a few short minutes since its beginning, already felt unchangeable and absolute.

Doubts would be cast aside.

Hesitation kills.

He would allow himself to be driven with such a rabid single-mindedness and a purity of purpose that it should have scared the hell out of him.

He asked her how are you feeling and he wanted to know, was there anything he could get her?

"God, I need a shower more'n anything..." She padded off to the bathroom, leaving him there, one step closer to the front door with his sweaty hands palming the car keys.

The spray of water drowned out most of what she was saying. He shoved the car keys into his pocket and stepped closer, just in time to catch the tail end of her thoughts.

"...real love, you know? Everlasting love. Eternal love."

He asked her to repeat herself, which she did.

"I said, for you to do what you did for me, it's just, well, it's gotta be something real. I mean, nobody's ever done anything like this for me before."

Which part did she mean? Taking her in? Killing a man? Letting her use the shower?

He nodded sympathetically and listened to Candace's story of how once, in junior high, a boy she

Collecting Candace

never liked tried to feel her up in assembly. When she wouldn't let him, he told stories about how nasty she was and how once in Social Studies he saw a spider crawl out from underneath her dress right in the middle of a pop quiz.

Come to think of it, she said, another boy came to her defense then too; he'd socked the liar in the nose.

"...broke it in two. Right in two. But I don't think he loved me. Least, not in the right way, I mean."

The water stopped as abruptly as it had started. She pushed the door open, holding a small Holiday Inn towel over the front of her body. The dirty blouse she had worn yesterday was tied around her hips, giving him a better idea of what he was in for. Her figure was softly rounded, but just thin enough to suit him. The blouse was tied low on her belly, and he could see her tummy protruding just a little, like a tiny beer belly. There were those damned blond hairs, all wet and matted together and just needing him to wipe them dry. He wanted to cup his rough hands over her, right there, and feel her easy, deep breaths.

Her long blond hair looked nearly black when it was wet and clinging to her cheeks and forehead. She stood before him in the hall, trembling a little and looking cold. When she spoke, the roughness was gone and the sound of her voice soothed that prickly feeling there on the back of his neck.

"What you said earlier, about fresh starts and all of that...I want you to know I'm for it, I am." She nodded firmly. Once, to affirm her commitment. "A hunnerd percent."

She shivered and shook a few drops onto the toe of his boots.

"I just wish..." She sighed, not really sure what she wished for. "Oh, hell...what good's wishing anyhow?"

She turned slightly, exposing a dark purple mass on her left shoulder blade. The way the design was formed on her skin, dense and thick in the middle and then lighter, more yellow than blue, around the edges, gave it a peculiar shape. He could probably see all kinds of things in it. Kind of like seeing ladies in rocking chairs or something like that, out of just the clouds. You had to kind of squint and use your imagination.

Candace noticed him studying her bruise. Her right hand came up and slung over her left shoulder, her middle finger reaching down to touch it lightly. It looked like it should hurt a hell of a lot, but her expression was blank and betrayed no sign of pain.

He should have felt pity, but if the truth'd been said, he'd have to confess that the sight of her bruise inspired him. Here was someone who actually needed salvation. All the martyrs he had known before, others who cried victim and suffered from persecution were just weak paranoiacs. He'd been summoned so many times, heard "wolf" cried more times than he could remember. None wanted his help, only his attention. None had needed him. None till Candace. It was a wonder that he had been able to recognize her cry for what it was, above the din of the rest.

She smiled, though not self-consciously. She pivoted her hips and let him see more. Grinning to himself, he remembered the way she flashed that god-awful tattoo.

How proud she must be when others think her brave.

She looked better already, and by her own account, felt better too. The bags under her eyes were almost gone, and when she giggled, or smiled even a little, he could hardly notice them there at all. The shower did it. The cleansing. He saw that the blood under her fingernails was gone and made a mental note to scrub the shower extra hard next time.

She changed the subject by flashing him a teasing smile and backing up toward the door, clutching the towel tighter and grasping for the knob behind her. Once she was hidden behind the door, her left hand came out and flailed blindly in the air until he guided the pile of clean clothes against her palm. She snatched them, giggled softly, and closed the door.

He tried to picture her face, but all he could see was the mark on her back.

It was late, and the inside of the house already reeked with the smell of his sweat. There was no use in opening any of the windows. There would be no wind. That heat wouldn't be going anywhere.

He headed out to the garage while Candace finished dressing. It was the coolest spot he knew of, what with the dirt floor and all. Even during the day, it was cooler than anyplace in the house, being situated under a tree. It didn't get unbearably hot in there till around one, when the sun would be a little to the west, just off center, and the heavy branches of the tree couldn't reach far enough to block it.

The smell of gas and oil in the tiny structure made it pretty hard to just sit quiet, but he knew it wouldn't smell as bad as Bobby Lee's place, all locked up tight and not a single window open to let the air in.

Christ, how it's gonna smell in there once the sun hits those windows.

He leaned against the makeshift workbench that ran the whole length of the eastern wall and lit a Vantage, but the lighted end warmed his nose when he took a drag so he flicked the butt onto the dirt floor and watched it burn itself out, till there was nothing but three inches of solid ash.

There was a small lamp on the workbench that lighted up the garage with a cool yellow glow when he switched it on. The slats that made up the walls of the structure were old and worn; the spaces between them in some places were wide enough to let a small field mouse in. Tonight, the only things that passed through were the rays of yellow light coming from inside, slicing up the dirt landscape on all four sides of the garage.

He remembered the way Candace looked when she came out of the shower. How he believed her when she said she felt good. He wished that he felt half as good. He hadn't had his shower yet, nor his meal, mostly 'cause of himself, mostly 'cause that's the way he wanted it. Like when you feed big dogs too much and they're no goddamned use anymore.

Besides, his sleep was shallow all night, fearful that she'd wake up hating him or wanting to go to the police. But he was wrong. She hadn't betrayed him. It was like she'd been nourished by the deed. Like she'd been wanting it. It seemed too simple when he had time alone to think things through like this. The answer was right there, written all over her face, and up and down the rest of her body too, if you took the time to notice. He couldn't believe some dumb bastard out there hadn't seen it first.

Contemplating murder was a lonely business. He thought it best if he stayed out there a while longer. Something up in the rafters caught his eye, a rat probably, rooting after something shiny of his, but when he walked to the center of the garage and strained his neck to look up he saw only the box. The Box. It had been so long since he'd thought about it, he'd almost forgotten it was there. Or maybe he'd hoped it would go away.

But it didn't. It was still sitting tight just where he'd left it nearly five years ago. Junk, his mother said. Crap that she wanted out of the house—probably love letters to other women. She wouldn't even look at it, she insisted he take it all. He did, but he never looked at it, either. Never was moved to, till today.

He placed an older ladder that didn't look like it would hold his weight up against the rafter and shook it once, judging its strength, and decided to go up there anyway.

Three rungs up it was probably ten degrees hotter than back down there on the floor, but he kept going.

In all the times he'd come out to the garage for a cigarette or some peace and quiet, he'd never once lifted his head and looked up there in those rafters. He knew The Box was there; he didn't have to look. He could feel it perched up there above his head, like some kind of fucking demon, grasping the rafter with talons, holding its breath and biding its time and just waiting for the right moment to swoop down on him and slit his throat. Ever since he'd stuck it up there after the funeral, he never liked to come into the garage, and if he absolutely had to, never walked under the rafters. Like how some dogs are afraid to go under bridges. Instinct.

He was mad at how he'd been tricked into noticing it this time.

His mother was right. It probably was full of love letters to other women. Snapshots of other kids. The parts of a life he wasn't allowed to know.

He'd thought of just pitching it into the river. He hated the way it sat up there and dared him to look up. To look inside.

And so up he went.

Once he got higher, the ladder shivered from his weight. It was hotter than anyplace in the world. He could feel the sweat pouring down his back and chest, could feel it under his jeans too, making the rough material chafe harder and more insistently with each rung he climbed.

Once at the top, he just stared at The Box. Just an old cardboard box with junk in it. He slapped the side once, trying to judge its weight. His hand came up and pinched one corner and lifted it a couple of inches off the beam where it had been resting peacefully for all this time; it weighed practically nothing.

Hoisting it up with one hand and grasping the ladder with the other, he lowered the weight onto his shoulder and began his shaky descent back to the ground. Things rattled around inside with his jerky movements, but it didn't sound like bronzed baby shoes or first footballs or any of the stuff that some other dad would keep.

Drenched with sweat and shivering from heat stroke, he sat on the lowest rung of the ladder and dragged the box over between his feet.

Written on the top in thick black Magic Marker was: DAD'S STUFF.

He wondered what was taking Candace so long and he wished that she'd get a move on.

He lit another cigarette, took a long drag, not even minding the heat from the tip, and placed it in the corner of his mouth. Squinting his eyes from the smoke, he leaned over and ran his palm along one smooth side, trying to feel its pull before even looking inside.

The memories were all there, crowded and cramped and using up all the space inside that little cardboard box. He wondered if his old man ever pulled that shit out of the closet, touching things, the way he touched the sharp contours of the cardboard. He wondered if he was the sort of man who liked to be reminded of little details like that, and if he used his touch to read these things like diaries. The smell, old and musty and dead, brought back the summers spent on the stoop, listening to his old man tell dirty jokes and loving the smell of Lucky Strikes on his clothes when he went up to bed.

The last summer, the best one, taking his first sip of beer from a bottle and hearing about pussy.

After that, their life together became a casualty of the times; a byproduct of woman's lib and the bomb and free love and linoleum kitchen floors. After that, all he could remember were stepbrothers and sisters and visiting the house just once but crying for two days straight till he was sent home to his mom.

He brought his other hand down and caressed the smooth, flat side before giving it a little push, lifting it two inches off the ground. Shaking it, he listened for clues, but there was just no telling what kind of shit his old man left behind. A fine dust covered his fingers as he traced a narrow, erratic path over the cool surface. He rubbed it into his fingertips and blew it away into nothing. Like ash.

He wished the bastard were there now, wished he could go to the grave and dig him up and beat the shit out of him, wished he could ask him how he let things get this far, how he let things tonight get this far and how come he wasn't there to stop him.

But he didn't know if his old man would be angry or what. Would he slap him down, holler at him, or wrestle him to the ground and muss up his hair, laughing, jabbing him in the belly and telling him to be a man.

Be a man.

Used to be a goal. Tonight, it was a curse.

He pulled on one of the loose flaps covering the top; the other three followed easily and the box was open. The contents stank something awful: liquor, dust, and that musty smell that memories get when you stick them away for a long time.

Lying on top was a small cowboy shirt. It was red and black with silver piping and chrome-plated snaps and it was all shrunk from being washed too much. He smiled as he lifted it out. The dark stain

Collecting Candace

across the front was barely noticeable, but he remembered that they'd taken it away from him just the same.

There were some baby pictures but they could have been anyone. It was hard telling babies apart and there were no names written on the back. He tossed them aside and dug deeper.

The heat attacked him from behind and he coughed, slapping his wet neck for bugs and trying to fan himself off a little.

There was stuff that belonged to the other family. This he tossed into a small pile on the dirt floor. There was a picture of his mother, when she was young and beautiful and in love, and he wondered if he'd ever look at Candace and see something other than his desire.

About two inches down, his fingers grasped the edge of some thick construction paper. It was an eight-and-a-half by eleven sheet, folded in half, the front covered with crude drawings of speedboats and army tanks and some silver glitter that was supposed to be sea spray. He laughed to himself, touched the front and accidentally knocked some of that glitter off.

Inside, a simple handwritten note in marker
I LOVE YOU DAD HAPPY BIRTHDAY
and surrounding it an almost perfect circle of old dried coffee, like beige watercolor. The paper was rippled where it had once been wet, and he tried to lay it on his knee and smooth it out but it had been over twenty years and it would never be fixed.

It was like finding a road map to the trip you took last year, where you got so fucking lost it ruined the whole vacation and now that map would be a whole lot of goddamned good.

He folded it again, into fourths, and stuck it in the back pocket of his jeans.

The rest of the stuff he let lie there in the dirt.

"I'm ready!" she hollered out the back window. Just in time. He didn't have to look toward the sky to know the sun was catching up to him. He stood and pushed The Box with the toe of his boot, leaving a fat, wide track across the dirt floor. He nestled it under the workbench and reached for the light; and in an instant, darkness swallowed up the garage again and he could hear the nighttime sounds of mice scratching across the floor, squeezing between the wall boards and coming out from their good hiding places. He pushed the door open and felt the first rush of fresh air; it felt good, coming out from inside that crypt.

The thick construction paper padded his back pocket as he slapped it once and headed for the house.

Two a.m. and at least a whole day ahead of them on the road. And on a day that would be hotter than any in recent history.

*　　　　*　　　　*

Seeing Candace's father added a whole other chapter to her life, and once the visit was over, it was easier to see the reasons—if there were any—for her life turning out like it had.

It was about three and way too hot for paying any kind of visit to anyone. He didn't want to go and would have said so right off if he'd known that's where she was headed, but she was driving and gave no indication that she was feeling in a family sort of way. He had dropped off to sleep before they'd even made their way out of town; no telling how long it was before he was awakened by the sound of gravel under the tires. He sat up straight in his seat and saw that they hadn't even hit the onramp yet. The digital clock that was stuck to the dash said 3:19. He'd been asleep for about seven minutes.

The humidity bathed his body all over but he tried hard as he could to ignore it.

It seemed strange that she wanted to see her father. Firstly, it was still the middle of the night, and from what he understood about her family, they were a churchgoing lot and might not look kindly on strange men before dawn. Secondly, in consideration of what they were on their way to do and all, it seemed to him that her dad would be the last one she'd want to visit; but he guessed it was probably no more queer than him taking a peek inside The Box. Only his time was cut short, and here she was, already pulling up to the house that she hoped would be hers one day.

It was set off some from the road down at the other end of a narrow gravel drive, which was crowded on either side by overgrown bushes and thick, drooping trees. The radials crunched loudly on the pebbles so Candace slowed the car down some, allowing him a little more time to check out this place in the light of the Maverick's headlamps. Raggedy branches slapped the windshield carelessly as the car squeezed through the narrow opening. That, and the sounds of nighttime creatures skulking off in the brush, made the whole thing feel wrong. But it was too late to turn back. Besides, the car wouldn't fit and they had to keep going.

Near the end of the drive was a large clearing, in the center of which sat Candace's dad's house. It looked small from the outside. One, maybe two bedrooms. It was typical of the kind of low-rent house he had always called home. Wood frame, one story. A long, wide porch fronted the house clear from one side to the other and looked useful for sitting out on hot, humid nights, as most were in this part of the country. That was the one thing they did right, them porches. The insides of these houses were like wool-lined coffins. Hotter than shit and no room to breathe.

Candace nudged the car a little to the right, and he could see a fat gray cat perched on a beat-up old chair up on the porch. It grasped the worn vinyl seat and arched its back up high, puffing itself up with fright. Its eyes gave off an iridescent yellow light that thrived on the illumination from the headlamps. It scared him some, so he made a loud hissing sound that sent that cat sprinting off into the woods.

Two windows with shades pulled stared out at them as they neared the clearing where the undiluted moonlight came down onto the roof of the house, lighting it up in some kind of fucking holy splendor. He smiled wryly to himself and figured well, hell, no wonder.

He half expected that front door to open up wide and for that house to swallow them whole, like those funhouses at the carnival where you ride the car straight up the clown's tongue.

Some strange life.

Candace slowed to a crawl once she had the front door in her sights. She leaned forward in her seat, hugging the steering wheel as she peered through the glass, surveying the blacked-out windows for something but finding nothing at all. The porch was crowded with used-up aluminum lawn chairs that sagged so bad in the seat they rested on the floorboards. Dozens of house plants fought for space, where there was any left; there were ones overflowing out of old Folger's cans, plants that sprouted dead flowers and some wild-looking things with no bloom at all but big vines that looked like arms the way they were stretched over the railings and around the legs of the chaise lounge.

On either side of the steps up the porch, two fat white columns, chipped and peeling and slouching under the weight of the roof, guided visitors like a portal to White Trash Hell. On the left column, a family of squirrels, painted real lifelike with brown fur and wide black eyes that stared into nowhere, were nailed up there so's it looked like they were all heading up to the roof for a picnic. On the right, three or four plastic blue jays had their feet screwed right into the wood. They looked silly, sticking straight out like coat hooks. Just beneath, nailed six inches or so below the blue jays, was a small crucifix.

Candace pulled a sharp right and then another and the car came to a sudden stop, turned around completely and now facing back the way they came in, toward the road.

He turned and peered back at the house through the rear window as Candace slipped her tennis shoes on, got out, and padded across the clearing toward the house.

He hated to see her go and wished she didn't have to.

A single bare bulb, maybe twenty-five watts, hung on an extension cord from the ceiling, dangling about six feet over the Astroturf welcome mat just in front of the screen door. Something was coming and he wanted to see what it was, but twisted all around like that, it hurt his neck so he settled rightways in his seat again and adjusted the rearview mirror so that he could watch her more easily.

It was funny seeing her like that, big as life in a piece of glass that was four inches by two. She was square in the center of the reflection, with a little bit of background on either side. That's all of her world he could see in the mirror. But that's all of her world there was.

She was right. He could smell that damned cereal milk all the way out in the drive.

He wasn't exactly sure where he was—too dark—but he knew that if he'd ever come this way before, it surely was on the way to someplace else.

Candace stood under the light bulb, which burned weakly, waiting up and watching for her.

He slid down into his seat and laid his head back on the headrest and adjusted the mirror, fixing her in his sights. He closed his eyes for a moment and listened to the screen door rattling on its hinges somewhere out there in the darkness. It was a homey, welcoming sound, the sound that kids listen for

Collecting Candace

when they're waiting on company.

He wondered why she'd left him in the car and why he wasn't the one up there on the porch, his hand extended and his face plastered in a silly, proud smile.

Hello, sir, I want to marry your daughter... Stop me if you've heard this one...

Was her old man gonna want to meet him at all? Pour him a drink? Was he gonna give him the talk about loving feelings and all that shit that he heard from neighbor kids 'cause his own dad had forgot?

Would her old man appreciate what was being done in the name of his daughter? Appreciate the lengths that some men might go to preserve that clean-smelling thing that he once bounced on his knee and tucked into bed? He chewed his thumbnail and watched her nervously, hoping he wouldn't see her signal for him across the drive, hoping that some six-foot-two bastard in a flannel night robe wasn't gonna come storming across that gravel clearing to yank him out of the car and check him out.

He looked out the window, tried to busy himself with the scenery but there was nothing out there to see. Just more of the same. More of Florida. He could hear her behind him, rattling the handle and calling out Yoo-hoo.

Company!

The sun would be on them in a matter of hours, and already he was suffocating from heat. His back was soaked and stuck to the seat, and he could feel a hot, damp rash developing on his thighs under his blue jeans.

He wiped the sweat from his brow and fine-tuned

the position of the mirror just in time to see the light switch off abruptly and Candace being swallowed up by the night. Just like he thought, when they first pulled into the drive. Evil clowns.

A small shaft of light came through from the inside when the door was pushed open, but it was low to the ground and lit up only their ankles. Hers, bare and smooth and taut, and someone else's, wrapped in acrylic socks on a hot night such as this. He stiffened in his seat and braced himself for the worse. He could hear their muted conversation somewhere in the night, her voice, childlike and soft, and another, flat and low and monotone. Whispers.

The screen door squeaked loudly and then slammed shut and when he looked into the mirror again, Candace had disappeared into the house. He noticed that she'd taken the car keys with her.

Getting pretty fucking hot all right.

He looked into the surrounding woods and tried to imagine them littered with state troopers, the tips of rifles with scopes and everything peering out through the bushes and pointed right between his eyes.

He fumbled in his seat and drummed the dash nervously with his fingertips, nails chewed down to the skin. Lord, she was taking a long time, whatever it was she was doing in there.

He began to sweat. Anxiety, fear, heat. Could have been anything. He wanted to get out of the car and stretch his legs, but knew that he'd have run clear to Texas if he'd been given half the chance. He felt trapped in the front seat of that Maverick, antsy, what with those thoughts of Bobby Lee and all. His mind went back to the Hi-N-Dri and he tried to re-member who was there that night, who might have seen him leave, who might have seen her, but nobody came to mind right off.

Suddenly his paranoia was cut short by a slap that rang as clear and loud in the Florida night as if he'd felt it himself. His face went hot and he spun around in his seat and waited for the next, he knew that there would surely be another; and once it came and he could determine where it was coming from, he pushed his weight into the car door and jumped out into the night. Upon standing up straight and pulling the crotch of his wet jeans away from his body, he immediately felt better. All thoughts of Texas had disappeared. Jaw set and fists clenched, he rounded the front of the Maverick just as Candace's voice came from inside.

"I'll be right out...."

Her voice had that eerie, sing-song quality, like she was trying hard to make like something was no big deal. He kept going and cursed the bastard under his breath. Under the watchful eye of the Lord he was being tested once again.

"Sit tight," she yelled out from one of the blank windows. "I'll be right out..." This she said with more emphasis, signaling for him to get back in the car and wait, which he didn't want to do. He stood under the moon and kicked at his shadow in the dirt, trying to hear what was going on in there and won-dering when this mission of God was going to end.

In another minute, Candace was flying out the front door and bouncing her way back for the car, waving her hands at him and motioning for him to get back in, which he did.

She pushed the door shut behind him and then thrust her head and shoulders in through the passenger's side window and asked for his address, but he was reluctant to give it right off like that. She'd been crying and even though she was making like she wasn't, her face was wet and streaked and what the hell did she think he would say seeing something like that? He straightened up in his seat and craned his neck to see back toward the house.

Fucking A....

She smiled weakly and wiped her face.

"Hot, ain't it?"

He palmed the door handle but just as he was about to yank it up she reached down and stopped him, grabbed his forearm, and told him to shush.

She stared at him blankly and shrugged her shoulders, as if to say What? It's my dad.

Why, he wanted to know, did she need the address? She'd been there, she'd seen where he lived, was she planning on sending him a postcard or what?

She smiled and threw him a kiss.

He remembered Bobby Lee's place and what a mess was still lying there and he wondered if anyone'd discovered the body yet. He wondered if Candace's old man ever bought Bobby Lee a drink and did he ever pull him aside and say man, she's a bundle of trouble good luck to you and then give him a playful slap on the face.

She asked him again and this time he gave her the number, and, after repeating it three times she bounded for the front door. He watched with regret

Collecting Candace

as she slipped out of reach and headed back for the house and he wondered if she'd ever come out of there alive.

Just as her feet hit the front porch, the screen door swung open and out, cutting off her path and stopping her in her tracks. A large man stepped out onto the porch, and though the darkness made it impossible to see his face, his manner and his personality were obvious in the way he stood before his daughter. He thrust his hand out, offering a little overnight bag, and in another two seconds, she was back in the car and pulling out of there and leaving him standing on the porch in his socks.

They looked back just as they pulled onto the road just in time to see the light flick back on. The man was gone.

A mile or so down the road she spoke.

"He's gonna miss me."

He just nodded. It was, after all, the next step.

chapter three

Danny Ray wouldn't die right off, and that made it hard.

It was plain from the start that things would be that way. Ever since Candace pulled her car onto I-75, things had gone haywire, and there was just no making up for it.

It was three-thirty and he was fully awake and ready for their road trip.

First thing, the radio broke. It was actually broke before they left for Decatur; some punk ripped the antenna right off the hood after Candace accidentally cut him off coming out of the 24-hour Taco Bell. The signal was strong in town, and it wasn't till they were probably twenty minutes on their way when static started popping from the right side door panel. The left speaker worked fine though, except they heard mostly just instrumentals, on account of the oldies station being the only one they could pick up with no antenna.

"Goddamngoddamngoddamn..." Candace would curse each time a new song began and she couldn't hear the words. He patiently explained to her over and over that it couldn't be helped, that that was just the way stereo worked, but that didn't stop Candace from fiddling with the buttons and screwing up what was left of the bass.

Collecting Candace

He didn't mind the music that way so much, but it pissed Candace off plenty. Her favorite thing was to sing along with the radio, but she didn't know the words to many of those older songs. She'd start off pretty good, she always got the beginning right, but sooner or later she'd start singing softer and slower and finally she'd just yawn or something, maybe pop a piece of Juicy Fruit into her mouth till the part she knew came back on. She tried to make it look casual, but he knew it was a bluff. He thought it was damn cute.

They drove all night and all morning like that, her humming and singing where she knew the words, him just putting up with it all. He had the gun shoved into his front pocket and it jabbed at him some, but was eased when he unbuckled his seat belt and stretched back a little. They didn't talk much; he tried to catch up on some sleep, but she drove too slow, even with nobody else on the road, and he was too impatient to sleep.

Some time around noon, when he thought they were getting close, he finally gave up on sleeping altogether. He reached up and switched the radio off completely just when "Venus in Blue Jeans" was begun for the seventh time since they left Gainesville. It was good timing; it was right about then that Candace was ready for lunch.

She pulled into the gravel parking lot of a roadside stand off the highway. A huge homemade sign said the specialty was chili dogs, but it was too hot for one of those, so he bought a coupla Cokes and a bag of boiled peanuts instead. He handed Candace her drink and leaned up against the door, taking care not to get jabbed where a piece of ragged antenna stuck out. The bag of peanuts was wet and warm, the liquid seeped out the bottom between his fingers as he lifted the weighty bag in the palm of his hand and offered some to Candace. She just shook her head and ambled away from the car, heading toward a late-model station wagon that was parked over in the shade. Some scruffy mutt was poking its wet black nose out a crack in the window, whining and sniffling when it saw her get out of the car. He shook his head. He knew how the dumb beast felt.

He watched her from behind as her shoes kicked up the dirt when she walked. The jeans he'd given her were loose and threadbare, pulled tight around the waist with a worn brown leather belt, but he could see parts of her body rubbing against the fabric when her muscles flexed underneath. She could be wrapped in burlap, and he could still make out the contours of Candace. It was like sonar or something.

It was even hotter than when they'd started out. His T-shirt was soaked right through with hot sweat. The smell of used oil and burned gasoline wafted over from the highway and just sort of settled on his head and shoulders. He peeled part of his shirt off his belly and it made this obscene sucking kind of noise as the fabric clung to his wet skin. He reached up under there with his Coke and pressed it flat against his stomach, but his body heat could have melted that ice in two minutes flat, so he took it away quick and flattened the wet shirt back up against his abdomen. He slapped it once, took a sip of Coke, and looked over at Candace, who had her whole body pressed right up there against that wagon, her lips pushing through the narrow opening at the top of the window and kissing that goddamned dog right on the nose.

He yelled across the parking lot, laughing, told her that dog licks its own butt, but she just giggled and flipped him off.

It was so easy to be with Candace. Doing those things for her, well, they didn't take too long, and once they were over, it would be just that much better between them.

They were just outside of Decatur, and had only a little ways left to go. With no radio or nothing. It was already one o'clock, Candace drove wild but she drove slow; he'd have had them there and back by now. He thought it'd be nice if they could find a room now, drop their stuff off and have someplace to go to right after. Someplace with a cool shower and a soft bed. It wasn't the same, wasn't as nice a trip as he could make it, but the main thing now was just getting there and then getting back.

He was watching Candace coo at the dog through the glass partition, just like wives do on visiting day, when a little blond thing of about five pushed through the screen door of the cafe, carrying a Styrofoam cup of water in one hand and a slushie in the other. Just as she passed through the doorway, a breeze caught on the screen and slammed it shut, scaring the poor thing and making her splash some of the water into the dirt.

She smiled at Candace, who lifted the child up to the window where the dog was panting for a drink. They fawned and fretted over that scrawny mutt like he'd never seen before.

He remembered the dog back at Danny Lee's place and he knew that if that little girl hadn't appeared when she did, it would've been just a few minutes before Candace sent him in with a paper cup. There was some saying about kids and dogs and how if they liked you well enough then you were sure to get into heaven; something like that, he couldn't remember exactly how it went, but he was glad to see both of them loving Candace. It said something for her.

The little girl had one of those boisterous, bossy voices that children get when they're trying to hold an adult's attention. But she didn't need to. Even after Candace had been told the dog's name (Buster) at least seven times, she didn't tell the girl to shush or anything. And when, for the eighth time, the child said it again, Candace, eyes wide with amazement and admiration, just said, "Yes, I know, that's a wonderful name!"

She petted one, then the other, and then waved back at him across the parking lot, and he knew she wished she could take them home.

He waved back and pointed at his watch.

Candace knelt down in front of the little girl, right there in the dirt, and smoothed her damp bangs back over her forehead, and the sight of it got him to wondering.

It could happen with her.

He could see her bouncing them on her knee, little bitty things just like that one, singing lullabies in that lazy, Southern way, and then shuffling them off to bed. He'd like to know that warm, damp smell of

Collecting Candace

babies on her skin and in her hair when it was time for bed. He'd known that smell once before—his sister's house reeked of it—but on Candace, it would be good. There was another one he remembered and thought about often, but that one was four and belonged to one of the women he'd known a long, long time ago.

He'd started out just trying to tolerate having a child in the house but ended up loving her all the same. When he split with her mom, he missed the little girl bad. For a while, he saw her every second Sunday. But it was never written down in court and when her mom took up with someone else, it got too complicated to visit anymore.

He knew that soon she'd forget him, like children are likely to do once you're out of sight for any length of time. He figured he'd get a page in the back of the photo album, there was that to be thankful for.

The dog whined from the backseat, smearing its nose all over and leaving wide tracks of snot across the window. Candace reached up and tapped the glass to try and hush it, but it only wanted to lick her fingers. She pushed them through the gap at the top and let them dangle there, and Buster licked them appreciatively.

He watched her loving that dog and knew she was lonely, probably right from the start, no matter how many times she'd been married or how many men told her they'd loved her. She probably had a whole pen full of stray animals when she was little, baby birds that couldn't fly–you had to be careful not to touch them, just in case the momma came back or else she'd kill 'em–and rats that were half-price at the pet store. She probably gave 'em all names too, like Mr. Whoosits, and probably ran home every day from school to play with them and tell them all her secrets. And when she got old enough for boys, he'd have bet that she kept a couple of pages of lined notebook paper hidden in the back of her math book–paper that was cluttered with flamboyant, childlike cursive, "Mrs. Bobby Lee, Candace Lee, Candace Lee, Candace Lee... Mrs. Danny Ray... Sincerely, Mrs. Danny Ray..." She probably had notebooks full of them, some in blue ink, some in red, furiously scribbled during lunch break or when the teacher's back was turned–those secret, soulful yearnings on some pre-pubescent's wish list.

His boots crunched in the gravel as he made his way for the cafe. The toes were covered with a fine dust of filth that kicked up around his ankles in little gusts when he walked. He cupped his hands and peered through the whitewashed screen door, but the little girl's parents were still leaning over the counter of the cafe, loading up on chili dogs and orange pop and rummaging for quarters to play some more Patsy Cline. He could see a rumpled old rag doll lying way back across one of the stools. Its cotton face was smeared with grape jelly that would probably never wash out.

He downed the last couple of peanuts and crumpled the wet bag in his hand, tossing it into the trash as he quickly made his way to Candace, the baby, and the dog. She was lifting the little girl up off the ground, giving her a big bear hug and a kiss on the cheek, not even noticing the purplish stains all over

Collecting Candace

the front of her—his—clean white shirt. His heart skipped a beat and he quickened his pace and broke into a trot and then slid up next to them, sending a shower of loose pebbles across their ankles.

In two minutes flat, the Maverick was out of there and doing eighty back on the highway. Before those folks even knew what hit them, they had lost their dog to Candace.

She hollered at him first, she even socked him in the shoulder a couple of times and cursed him pretty bad too. But when she laid their clean clothes out on the back seat for that mangy mutt, he knew he'd done the right thing, no matter what she'd have him believe.

They got away clean; and he could tell that Candace was happy to have the dog with her. It was nice to give her something, it was nice to please her, but even he knew that it really was like starting off on the wrong foot and he swore to himself that he'd try not to do that again. Besides, now his windows were fogged up and dirtied with those runny, whitish streaks.

It was getting hotter the further north they drove. The Blessed Virgin Mary was looking kind of peaked, like plastic statuettes are gonna do when they're exposed to hot sunlight like She'd been. He hoped She wouldn't start melting all over the dash; Candace was sure to lose her religion then, and, besides, he'd come to be fond of the tiny Mother of God. In a way, it was all 'cause of Her that he was there with Candace. She was partly to blame for everything. But now Her eyes were all drooped and the corners of her mouth were down-turned, and there were tiny tidepools of flesh-colored paint on her cheekbones. She was looking pretty sorry now.

The heat had finally gotten to the dog too; it was curled up on the floorboard under Candace's feet, panting and dragging its tongue, like dogs do when they're having a hard time sleeping. The stupid beast didn't even have enough of a brain to realize it was ten degrees hotter down there near the engine and a cooler spot would've been in the back where she'd laid a bed out and everything. But the dog didn't care, it only wanted to be close to Candace. Didn't matter how hot it got.

There wasn't much to say through most of southern Georgia. He thought she must be thinking about Danny, being on the way to see him and all. It was all he could think about too, but he was glad that she wasn't wanting to talk about it.

After a long period of silence and counting the mile markers, Candace finally did speak, but the story she told was only indirectly about her second husband.

"The man at the agency said I was a natural," she said, sighing as she looked out the window. "He said that not too many girls could make a good living at figure modeling... but I could... anyway, that's what he said."

He didn't know for sure what figure modeling was.

"Well," she began, rummaging through her bag, "it's just like regular modeling, okay? Only..." she popped her gum and pulled out her wallet and flipped through some old receipts and bits of paper with phone numbers written on them. "Only...

ha! Here it is..." She pinched the corner of an old slide between her fingers and held it up to the light. "...here it is..." Her peach-glossed lips formed a tight O and she blew the dust off the negative. It looked pretty ratty and the white border was starting to peel away from the film. "...only you don't wear any clothes..."

He held out his upturned palm, motioning for her to drop it in his hand and when she did, he stared at her blankly.

"Get it? Figure modeling... you model your figure, you know? Nekkid..." She giggled lewdly and blushed, dropping the slide into his hand.

He moved the car over to the right lane and slowed it a little so he could take a quick look at the slide of her naked body. Probably should have stopped the car altogether but it was another mile and a half till the exit.

The slide was small, only an inch square, but the bright sun reflecting through the windshield lit it all up from behind and made it pretty easy to see her clear enough. She looked pretty much the same as she did sitting next to him—at least, the parts he recognized did—so it was hard telling how long ago it was shot.

He thought it looked very professional, especially with the palm tree in the background.

"That's real sand, can you tell?"

He could.

She was kneeling and was naked except for a pair of ruffled white anklets, holding a bright red beach ball up against her belly and looking seductively into the camera. Her long blond hair was all done up in two pigtails that made her look younger–that, and the socks.

"Don't ask me why I'm wearing socks..." She held her hand up in the air. "'Cause I don't know...you don't think it ruins the picture, do you?"

He didn't.

"Jesus only knows what that man was thinking."

He thought about the photographer setting up the shot, getting a naked woman like that in his sights and then putting some goddamn socks on her. He couldn't figure it out either, guessed it was probably some kind of temporary insanity.

"Watch out!" she shrieked, leaving him only seconds to jerk the Maverick over back to his side of the road and pull it onto the sloped shoulder. The blaring wail from an eighteen-wheeler drowned out his mumbled curses and then died gradually as the trucker barreled on past them. The driver thrust his left arm out the window at the last minute and flipped them the bird.

"ASSHOLES!"

They sat in silence for a moment, waiting for the pounding to go away; Candace's from fright, and his from a sudden rush of blood throughout his whole body. His left hand clutched the steering and his right, the slide, now damp with his perspiration.

"My goodness..." She whistled. Even the dog had woken up.

She smoothed her hair back and he pressed the slide up against the windshield to get a better look.

There she was. Naked, that's for sure. He could feel the drops of sweat creeping down the back of his

Collecting Candace

scalp and sliding into the collar of his shirt.

Lord, it is hot.

He tried to imagine the exact moment when the photographer snapped this particular photo. Was she in a good mood that day? Had she just eaten lunch or was her stomach rumbling? Was she as accommodating as she seemed in the picture, all spread legs and wide-open arms, or was it just another job?

He had the picture. He held it in his hands, but the moment wasn't there. Someone else got it, and kept it.

It was Danny's idea for Candace to get into figure modeling. One of his buddies had a girlfriend who made a pretty steady income off of posing for girlie magazines. Danny must have thought that it was pretty easy cash for a guy like himself.

The way Candace described it, it seemed that someone oughta be doing time for making her do things like that. Though she swore that she never done nothing dirty and was not ashamed of herself, though others might be, it was still hard to hear about her doing such things.

Most of her money came not from actually posing for the camera but from her auditions. Candace booked lots of auditions, up to three a day. She'd call her agency every morning, "just like a real model does," and get her calls for the day. It never seemed suspicious to a girl like Candace that her prospective employers, casting agents, were checking her out in cubicle offices of manufacturing companies and private living rooms. She never even batted an eye when some wheezing middle manager locked his door and asked her to strip.

He slipped the slide into his shirt pocket and pulled back onto the highway, just catching the tail-wind of one of those big chrome gasoline trucks.

He watched their reflection in the rear panel of the Exxon tanker; he liked the way it made the Maverick look. Like it was eating up the asphalt. He liked watching the places they'd been disappear fast, all that shit back there. Every ten feet or so another chunk of it would seem to just slide right off the earth behind them. The world seemed wide open in that shiny chrome; it seemed smaller too, like it wasn't so far to where they were trying to get to. In practically no time at all they were there.

By the time they got to Decatur, Candace was tired and Buster was whining. It was hard carting around a girl and her dog, it was a longer drive than he thought it would be, and he knew he wouldn't feel much like killing a man once they pulled into town.

He knew there was no use doing any goddamn thing at all in the shape he was in. There weren't nothing coherent going on at all above the waist, not with an image like hers still in his brain and her picture still in his pocket.

There were lots of motels in town they could hide out in, but it took almost forty-five minutes to find one that Candace liked. It was a rundown string of cabins all hooked together in an upside down U that circled a dusty parking lot. There was a pool in the back, but the plaster was bleached white and cracked and faded and there probably hadn't been water in it in twenty years. That didn't stop them from juicing up that neon sign every day, though, and that was what attracted Candace in the first place.

Collecting Candace

It was a swimmer, outlined in blue neon and poised on the edge of diving board, and even when the Maverick passed underneath the sign on the way back to their room they could hear the loud sizzling of neon tubes. Candace was awestruck as she watched a second pass and the swimmer now airborne, his back rounded and his head down. Next his feet were straight up in the air and he was heading straight for that dried-out pool. The sign sputtered laboriously and now he was gone, swallowed up by the blue waves of electrified neon.

The cycle took about five seconds to complete, and it captivated Candace. After it was done, the swimmer would find himself up on that board, ready to do it all over again. It was like that book he'd read about Hell where you gotta walk this circle, only you're all chopped up and your body is in pieces and you gotta get yourself back together; but just when you do that—your legs connect with your torso and your arms are back in place and you complete one revolution—you get all hacked up again and gotta start from the beginning. And that's what you do forever. Just like that swimmer. Just like him.

They got a tiny room near the back. It had a view of the pool, smack in the center of the U-shape, which would make it easy to see if someone was coming down that drive. They got out of the car and stepped into the blinding Georgia day. The parking lot, a mixture of rocks and white sand, shone brightly in the sun and he had to shield his eyes from the reflection. There were no trees or nothing to break up the sunlight, and over where the empty pool sat it was even brighter.

He stepped up to number eleven and jammed the key in, turned it once, and kicked the door open while Candace fumbled with getting their belongings out of the backseat of the Maverick.

It smelled terrible, like it hadn't been opened in years, even though the cleaning lady had been there recently, as evidenced by the frilly paper covers on the drinking cups that sat with the plastic ice bucket on the bureau. Two twin beds took up most of the space in the room. One was covered with a worn, white chenille bedspread, and the other had a gaudy, flowery-patterned comforter. Nothing matched the drapes, which were a sort of threadbare mesh, colored a deep rust.

The bathroom was small but adequate, and Candace squealed when she got to push her hand through the paper seal over the toilet seat, loving it so much, like she was launching a fucking battleship or something.

There was a small indent in the wall that was supposed to be the closet. He could tell because of the splintered dowel that hung there, sagging in the middle. Good thing they had nothing on hangers, for it looked like they'd have to just stuff them into a drawer anyway.

Beside the closet was another sink. No mirror, nothing else. Just a little sink.

There was nothing to put away, no toiletries and the change of clothes was left in the car. There was just the gun, which he laid in the nightstand drawer, right on top of the Bible. Candace moved it down underneath, with the Yellow Pages. He didn't mind.

He crashed and Candace watched some TV. And

that's the way they stayed for the next five hours or so, like vampires, waiting for dusk.

When he woke up, he gave himself no time to think of anything, not the heat, which was no longer mindful of any previous records and was now headed straight for the fucking ceiling; not the girl; not even the smell of dog pee in the room. He got up, loaded the one bullet, washed his face and herded them into the car.

He thought of his father as he turned the ignition key. Wondered what kind of a man he really was and wondered for what reason the folded-up birthday car in his back pocket was saved.

They didn't speak on the way over, and about five blocks from Danny Ray's house, he pulled over, shut off the engine, and settled back into his seat. It was almost midnight, and most everyone in the neighborhood was asleep. Those who weren't were likely dead drunk and wouldn't notice them anyway.

It took a couple of minutes for the noises under the hood to die down, but he was in no hurry. And, anyway, those random clicks and pings, he liked the sound of them, final in some way. Sounds of a journey coming to an end.

But he knew that wasn't true, and suddenly it occurred to him that he probably shouldn't have shut off the motor at all; might not start up again. He turned the key once and when the engine sputtered to life, turned it off again just as quick, satisfied that they could get on with things once they were ready to.

There was a dog barking somewhere off down

the block, wanting to be let in.

It was hard to see out the front window, what with all the trash cluttering the dashboard and that little plastic thing and all. Besides, there were huge white streaks of snot that made it impossible to see anything in the dark. He leaned forward and breathed once on the biggest white spot of all, then rubbed the glass clean with a napkin from the Dairy Queen.

The neighborhood was rundown some; lawns were cluttered with rusted out mini-bikes with no wheels and old v-dubs, good cond, no eng, no trans. One of them had FOR SALE painted across the windshield in soap. U pick up.

He figured most of the guys on that block, maybe even Danny Ray, were just regular guys, probably a little more ordinary than himself.

He guessed it didn't look like the type of place where people gave a shit what you were doing as long as you stayed over on your own property and didn't let your guests piss on their lawns.

There was a big old boat blocking one driveway down at the end of the block. He smiled to himself. Every block he'd ever lived on there's some asshole with a boat. You gotta kiss his ass and buy him beer and get your wife to babysit his smart-aleck kids—and his kids are always the worst—if you ever wanna go fishing on that boat. He's the big shot on the block, till some other fucker goes and buys a jet ski. Dog-eat-dog, ain't it.

He could feel the gun in his front pocket, prodding him insistently. It had been nudging the inside of his thigh ever since they left Gainesville and he'd worried the whole way up about shooting his balls off.

Fat chance.

Candace was sitting beside him, her forehead resting gently on the window. She was awake though drowsy and singing the parts that she knew to an old Frank Sinatra song.

"When somebody loves you..."

Her breath fogged up a small areas of glass, and when it got thick, she touched her fingertip to the mist and traced a near-perfect drawing of a heart with an arrow through it. She sang some more

"...it's no good unless he loves you..."

The mist started to disappear, so she breathed heavily into the last few words.

"...allll the wayyyy...."

She traced "CH &" into the heart, but there wasn't room for anything else.

Yep, still in there.

He was still in the middle of falling in love, still in the thick of it and watching things like this only made it harder to slow down. He remembered thinking when he first saw this one, the first thought he had was that he loved her. The second was that he didn't want to know nothing about her. He wanted to just love her like that, simple-like.

Private jokes and farting by accident and then laughing so hard you gotta do it again–things like that sound so stupid when you talk about 'em, but he knew that it was that kind of stuff that made it hard to think of anything else when she wasn't around.

He thought of Lord-knows-who sitting out there in that quiet Southern night, clutching a Pabst and rocking on the porch and bragging, "Man, that Candace. I can remember things about her..." They'd chuckle knowingly, wink at one another and then say, "...Hell, you gotta love her."

All the way.

"Why'd the monkey fall out of the tree?"

She giggled and slipped her left foot underneath her right thigh, sitting half Indian style and leaning over closer to him. It was dark in there, but just past her silhouette he could see the light from the streetlamp reflecting in the sweaty smears where the heart used to be.

He didn't know what the fuck she was talking about.

She took a sip of warm, flat Coke and said it again. "Why'd the monkey fall out of the tree?"

He shrugged.

Candace's lips were pursed in a tight smile. Even in the darkness he could feel her excitement in that car. She was getting all red and flushed and 'bout to damn near bust. Finally she could take it no more.

"'Cause it was dead!" she squealed.

He didn't want to laugh, 'cause it was a stupid joke. It didn't make no sense to him, but she was having a hell of a time with it, repeating the punch line over and over, laughing harder each time even though she knew damn well what the answer would be.

"'Cause he was dead," she snickered to herself and sighed.

Moments passed, it was quiet and he didn't know what to say. She turned to look at him, still grinning from ear to ear. "Get it?"

That made him laugh, which sent her into a fit of giggles all over again.

Dead monkeys and dogs with no legs. Candace sure was something.

They didn't talk for a few minutes, both of them sat there and pictured some poor fucking dead monkey falling out of a tree, and that would set them off all over again. Gradually, their laughter turned into little snickers and gasps, and then just broad smiles. And just when the good time was about ready to die down altogether, Candace turned away and spoke up.

"I guess a lot of people think I'm pretty dumb. I know what's going on. I know what's happening. You think it don't bother me? Is that what you think? That it don't bother me?"

He wasn't sure what kind of effect any of this—Bobby Lee, Danny Ray, the dog, the heat—had on her.

"'Course I feel bad. A person wouldn't be human if they didn't feel something. Hafta be some kinda robot or somethin'." She folded her hands in her lap and picked at the loose threads on the fringe of a tear in the jeans. "I feel things. I know."

Do you love me, Candace?

He couldn't bring himself to say it, but he thought it real hard for a few minutes, hoping that she'd hear him.

"I try not to think hard on bad things is all."

He nodded.

"It's like I said back at the house, I'm with you a hundred percent." She was silent again, most likely thinking about Danny Ray and the last time she saw him. Maybe she was wondering if things were really so bad after all.

"I don't wish nobody no harm. And I ain't got a revengeful bone in my whole body, really."

He believed the words but wondered if she was convincing herself, or was she trying to look good in the eyes of the Lord or whoever else might be listening.

"All's I've ever done is wrong. But it ain't 'cause I'm stupid, 'cause I'm not, you know. And I ain't no whore either. I know a lot of people think that, on account of me having had three husbands."

He wanted to hold her hand but just pressed his cheek against the warm glass and wondered when the fucking heat would break.

"I only slept with three men in my entire life, that's the truth." She paused. "It's just the way I am, I guess. Down-to-earth is what they call it. Old-fashioned." She looked down at her hands, her chewed-up nails and cuticles and shrugged. "I dunno."

He nodded. She spoke the truth.

"I'm twenty-six and a half, and I ain't never been to a funeral. That's pretty good, ain't it?"

It was getting late. It was fine to sit and talk, but their legs were stiff and they wanted to get on with it and get back home soon as possible.

Candace pointed through the windshield. "Two blocks up and then two more to the right. I'll show you where."

He started the car, half hoping that it wouldn't kick up, but it did. After he made the right, he dimmed his lights and used only the parking lamps.

'Cause it was dead.

Collecting Candace

He laughed to himself. It was very late, and very hot.

chapter four

Time was, being a regular guy was a good thing. That's a lesson he learned from his dad. With mediocrity came a sense of sameness, of stability and safety. Things that guys strived for and women sought. It was a funny world then, when you could brag about nothingness and others would envy it.

Maybe it wasn't the times after all. Maybe it was him. Maybe lack of ambition wasn't really peace of mind. Maybe it was just laziness. He didn't know anymore. Didn't really matter anyway, but he thought of it just the same, the solace in knowing that should all else fail, at least he could still be a regular guy.

These days, there wasn't much noble about plastic dishes and a beat-up old car.

This and more crowded his brain right before he squeezed off the first and only shot that he hoped would kill Danny Ray dead as a bug in the drive.

Candace was afraid to stay downstairs alone, she wanted to stick close. He knew it was a mistake to let her in the bedroom with him; before, she'd gotten smeared with blood, and this time he'd brought only one fresh change of clothes. He meant to push her out the door right before he got down to it, but she slid quietly inside behind him. Yelling at her or getting pushy would have just woke Danny Ray up.

Collecting Candace

At first, he could hardly tell she was there, except for when her breathing got heavy.

It was black in the bedroom; it was nothing all around him. In the time it took his eyes to adjust to the dark, he just stood stock still, his back pressed against the wall and his ears pricked up for the sounds of the two of them breathing.

He was scared to death that Danny Ray would wake up. That he'd hear something, one of those nighttime sounds that wake you out of even the deepest sleep.

Maybe that was what he really wanted anyway
No
but hell he didn't know what he wanted anymore. Only now that he was finally poised on the edge of success, it was natural to wonder if there maybe weren't some other way that'd been overlooked. But Danny Ray lay there, primed and prone and ready to take it like a man.

Things were working on them two, on him and Danny Ray, things that she had told the both of them were in that room on this night, bringing the three of them all together in the most frightening, final way. The stories, all the firsts that Danny Ray had hoarded for himself. Stupid things, like the first time she ever ate guacamole. (She didn't like it.) Bigger things too, like the first poem she ever wrote, addressed to Danny Ray.

My arms are open
but my fingers they bleed
come to me my love
to be wrapped up in need
He heard her soft whisper just before the shot

rang out—a chant, a prayer, whatever. A curse would have fit nicely. He didn't know what it was, himself, not being Catholic and all, and it sounded Catholic-like, but he knew she wasn't reciting the Lord's Prayer or anything like that. That would have been too easy, and if there was one thing that Candace wasn't, it was easy.

She might have been telling him to be careful, probably was telling him to get it right. After all, he'd brought only one bullet. That said a lot. Mostly he liked the way it just said Fuck You. But when he saw the flash of powder and saw Danny Ray do that twitching thing, he wasn't thinking Fuck You. Pleasediepleasediepleasedie, was all he could put together.

Course Danny Ray didn't die. Not right away, like he should have. First the antenna, and now this. Some people have no luck.

It had gone smoothly the first time, with Bobby Lee and the baseball bat. It was messy, but it was fast. And he supposed it was just taken for granted that he'd be just as adept the second time.

Danny Ray was lying on his side, the whole right side of his face buried in the pillows but the left just as inviting as it could be. Easy target, like them cans of Bud. He stepped up closer and pointed the barrel right at Danny's temple. And what if he got it wrong?

Do-over.

Not this time.

Get out of there, stupid fuck.

Danny Ray didn't move. Some folks don't have no sense, not to come in out of the rain, not to do nothin'. He thought of the time he was eight and a neighbor boy got his head run over by the S&P. They were all hanging out down by the tracks and this one smart kid said he could tell if a train was coming by laying his head on the tracks and listening for the vibrations.

He was right every time. It was a neat trick, except one day when the band of his wristwatch caught on a rusty old nail in the tie, and he couldn't get out of the way fast enough. All the other boys ran away, hid behind the cardboard shacks and empty oil drums. He stood there though, watched the whole thing. Couldn't have been standing more than ten feet away. Ruined his cowboy shirt, the red one with silver piping and real chrome-plated snaps. She washed it nearly a million times but it never did no good. He never wore it again.

It was like that now, Danny Ray laying there, sleeping in the path of this bullet, sleeping on the tracks like a stupid fuck.

Wake up!

There was lots of time to change his mind. To wake Danny up, get out of there before things really got out of hand. But she was there too, somewhere in the darkness with him. She was behind him, so he couldn't see her, but he could feel her. Smell her too and it was more than enough of a reminder why he was there in the first place.

She might even hate him. At first.

There was the slide in his pocket and he thought about how fucking hot it was in that room right then, just like it would have been at the beach where that guy took that photo. Only it was a studio where she posed naked and it probably wasn't hot at all. Not like this. Nothing was ever hot like this.

Could she hate me for such a thing?

He wiped the sweat from his face and cocked the gun, easing the hammer back and thinking to himself well now things are surely set in motion.

I got the dog. I did do that.

As bad luck would have it, Danny Ray rolled over just before the hammer struck. Must've been having a bad dream or something; Danny ended up on his back, and since it was too late to stop it now, the bullet had to just go and find its own path.

It hit him high in the forehead, way up by his hairline, and came out through the top of his head, lodging itself in the wall behind the bed.

Goddamnmotherfuckingsonofabitch

All that build-up and for what? Hardly seemed to wake the bastard.

Candace screamed. Then she turned on the ceiling light.

Things were not going well.

There was a mess like they'd never seen anywhere. Behind Danny Ray's head and covering a section of wall maybe four foot long and three foot high was an explosion of the deepest, wettest shade of red he'd ever seen. There was hair too and pieces of skin and instantly it made him want to puke but Candace couldn't get past the sight of that head upon that pillow.

Danny Ray's eyes were wide open, his mouth too, and his hand came up to his forehead. It must've been a rude shock to feel the blood and the hole there. He was speechless.

Collecting Candace

It was clear from the look on Danny Ray's face that he'd totally forgotten about the figure modeling.

Pain like that was hard to imagine.

"...Sweet Mother, I place this cause in your hands..."

He hoped she was praying for the poor fuck to die fast.

Made a fine mess of everything.

He couldn't remember how'd they executed that man last summer. He remembered seeing them on the news, strangers that come from far away as the West Coast, lining the road up to the pen, some standing, some sitting in little beach chairs with their sleeping bags and thermoses of coffee. It was only five a.m. and already they were there in hordes, shouting at the newsmen and holding up signs that said, "He'd rather die than switch."

Candace could not take her eyes off of Danny Ray. He recognized her right off—she hadn't changed that much after all—and he tried to speak her name but blood was the only thing that would come out.

She screamed again and it was bad.

They'd been in the house only five minutes, and he had already fucked up beyond belief. It was a bad scene, good intentions aside.

The road to hell has surely never been paved with anything like this before.

From the way that Candace looked, the color of her skin and the black in her eyes, he guessed that she was in shock. Small wonder, with what she'd seen. And now, making things worse, that half-dead ex-husband of hers lay there, reaching out for her with one bloody hand and plugging up the bullet hole with the other.

She made a motion like she was gonna step closer to the bed, like she was gonna touch that bastard. Whatever in the world she wanted to touch that man for was a mystery for sure. Only he was dying, not fast, buy dying just the same, and she seemed to wanna lay her hands on his breathing body just one more time.

Feel the life. Let Jesus show you how.

Her hand came out, her middle and forefinger dangled like she was heading for a hot stove, but she was stopped halfway. Her path was blocked. He stepped between Candace and her ex-husband and he tried to shake her out of it, but she was in deep. He slapped her once and she cried and then she spat on him. She spat right in his face.

It was all of it. The sight of her, afraid of him and ashamed and what did she need to turn that fucking light on for, anyways? And Danny Ray himself, he wasn't helping any. The way that corpse lay behind him there on the bed, whispering Candace's name through reddened teeth like he was speaking some kind of blasphemy, beckoning her forward. And for what? A last kiss, or did he just want to get her close enough so that he could slip his fingers around her throat and take her with him?

It was unbearable. He began to cry. There was no control. There was no one in charge.

He pushed Candace back through the door and slammed it in her face and locked it, and then swung around to set things right again.

Collecting Candace

He scanned the room for something heavy, but there was nothing but a tiny ceramic lamp on the nightstand, and that would hardly raise a bump.

The gun in his hand was slick with sweat, and he wished to God–Candace's God–that he'd brought another bullet.

As he threw himself onto the bed and straddled Danny Ray's chest, he slapped the gun into his right hand and held the man's head still with his left. Danny Ray proceeded to voice his objections but he didn't pay any mind 'cause the garbled shit that came outta that man's mouth meant nothing at that moment. That bastard had had his say in regards to Candace long ago.

He dug his knees into the dying man's sides. It wasn't rage that finally sent him over, though it could have easily done so any time up till now. It wasn't fear or want for Candace or any of those things that drove him out of the Hi-N-Dri's parking lot and all the way up I-75 in the first place. It wasn't that slide in his pocket or that gelatinous Mother of God on the dashboard of the Maverick. Wasn't none of that second Sunday shit neither. It was the heat.

It's the heat that makes people crazy, makes 'em up and kill everyone in the house. Summertime's when most people snap, he knew that to be a fact. Summertime, and Christmas. People can only take so much.

The sweat dripped off his face and onto Danny Ray's, falling in the poor bastard's eyes and probably stinging him too.

Christ, it was hard to get a break.

He brought the gun butt square down onto Danny Ray's chin; the bone gave way underneath and blood splattered everywhere and he had to turn his face real quick to the side so as not to get some in the eye. Another left. Then another and another. He pounded Danny Ray's face till it felt all soft and rubbery like there was nothing left and when his hands became too slick to hold onto the gun, he shoved it into his jeans pocket and reached over for the clock radio and used that.

It was taking so long. It should have been over and done with ten minutes ago but Danny Ray was taking so fucking long. There was this voice screaming no, no, stop it, please, and he was scared at first and then relieved to know the voice was coming from the other side of the door and not from inside of himself. Candace was banging on the door and making an awful racket. He didn't know if she wanted him to stop, or if she just wanted to see, so he kept going. He was almost done anyway.

He pounded the body some more.

He thought of the dream. The same one. Gray bars, gray uniform, a stiff cot. He could feel it, narrow and hard, unyielding beneath his sobbing body. He lay all curled up on his side, his knees drawn to his chest and his face buried in his hands. He tried to sink into the blanket, to blend with the mattress, but there was no hiding from himself. He had killed a man. He didn't know who, or when, but he could feel it. The aftermath of murder inside that tiny room with a sink, a toilet, and some photos taped to the wall above his bed.

It was the only recurring dream he'd ever had, and the only one that came with colors and sounds

and smells. It was bigger than life, as so many trag-
edies are. And the desperation and hopelessness that
wanted to suffocate him rose up all around and
pushed his face down into the rough, scratchy blanket. None of that wake-up-on-three crap this time.
This was real. This was life. Life behind bars.

And then things would take a turn for the worse.
He would wake up. He'd sit up in bed sobbing,
clutching a soaked pillow to his chest and gasping
for air as he tried to pull himself out of the muck
of his subconscious. Just a dream, just a dream,
he'd tell himself over and over and over. And then
he'd laugh. Fear and relief, mostly relief, tinged his
laughter as he began to fully rouse himself from the
bad dream.

But goddamn if it didn't happen again. He'd sit
up in bed and throw his legs over the side, expecting
to kick one of the sleeping cats, but instead he'd feel
the cold concrete under his toes and the bony cot under his ass. Back in his cell, he'd do it all over again,
like that fucking Twilight Zone or something. More
crying, maybe suicide. Then, in a sarcastic twist of
fate, he'd wake up at Denny's over a cup of decaf,
wiping the sweat from his brow and leaning over the
table to tell his best friend about these weird fucking dreams that he's been having. And so he'd go
all night. Only seconds, minutes, according to those
dream books he checked out of the library, but he
could swear that he'd aged at least five years a night
since the dreams started.

The ones that used to live with him complained
that he'd wake up screaming three, four nights
a week. Some would kick him out of bed, others

would just leave him there and go away. There was never anyone to hold him and to tell him it was just a dream. It should have been just a dream. It should have stayed that way.

He pounded Danny Ray's body some more till some tiny plastic bits chipped off the radio and hit him in the eye. And that was when he knew he'd had enough.

Sobbing and soaked with sweat, he rolled off the bed onto the carpet, clutching the broken, bloodied alarm clock to his chest. The gun dug into his groin when he hit the floor, and the full weight of his body fell onto his knees, which popped under the pressure.

The carpet was thin and scratchy under his palms as he crawled for the door. That light. That fucking light was still on and he could see the blood. Everywhere. On him, on the walls, on the floor. He crawled on all fours. Scurrying quickly across the carpet, he looked over his shoulder and saw the red stain spread and he moved faster. There, next to the door was the switch that she had flipped on, four feet off the floor. He dove for it, smearing the hollow core door with blood and sweat and grime and in an instant, it was dark again.

Candace was out there still. She was rapping on the door and calling him over and over and saying please come out and dragging her knuckles across that hollow core door. The noise went clickety-clack 'cause of all those silver rings on her fingers. She was calling his name and wanting to see him, to see that he was all right. It wasn't Danny Ray that she was calling for, she never once mentioned Danny Ray's name, and that was what made everything that had happened all right.

He opened the door with some difficulty, on account of his wet and slippery palms, and found her standing straight up against the back wall, her knees locked and her shoulders pressed against the awful wallpaper. Her bare toes tapped the carpet aimlessly, like she was feeling pouty or something, but she didn't appear to be doing that. It was dark, but there was a faint mist of moonlight creeping in through the big picture window in the living room and up the stairs, and he could see her pretty clear. She looked tired. And hot.

He had fully expected to not find her there at all. He could just as easily have looked out the front window and seen her running down the middle of the street, screaming for the police and praying for Jesus to deliver her from evil.

He'd told her it was no place for a girl. Now, he was sure she was gonna have plenty to say. After all, a sight like that stays with you a long time.

They just looked one another over. She seemed not to notice the blood on his hands, nor on his shirt nor on his face. She was looking past, through the door and into the mess that he'd just crawled out of, but he pulled the door closed behind him and stepped closer, causing her to react like a skittish colt when he came near.

He moved slowly, fearful of scaring her off. He hoped to God that she wouldn't start to cry 'cause he knew that if she did, he'd be unable to stop his own fitful tears.

"I'm sorry." Her voice was soft and sorrowful

and even though that's all she said, he hesitated before saying anything back for he was sure she was gonna tack a "Daddy" on there at the end.

She didn't.

She reached for him, dangling her fingers there and making motions like she wanted him to take them, which he did. Her hands were dry and cool, but, once having made contact with his, became just as slippery and wet. Nobody said anything about it, even though they could feel it, warm and thick, making it hard for them to get a good hold on one another. He laced his fingers into hers and pulled her away from the wall and closer to him, just so her chest grazed over his, and then he let go of her. She still wouldn't look him in the eyes, and he was sorry he'd slapped her, even if it was for her own good.

She probably did hate him, all things considered.

Candace stood swayback in front of him, and slipped her hands into her back pockets.

There go them clean clothes.

"Forgive me?"

He never would understand women.

He pushed past and tugged on her fingers for her to follow. It hurt when she touched the parts of his hands that were scraped and bruised from beating on Danny Ray so bad. He winced when her thumbs pressed into the raw, open cuts on his knuckles.

"It's so damn hot in here, ain't it?" she whispered. Her voice was trembling and sounded kind of funny, but he ignored it.

It was one-thirty. He thought about stopping in the kitchen to wash up, at least to splash some cold

Collecting Candace

water on his face and neck–he did that last time and it was okay–but this time, the thought of being in the house with a man who was so thoroughly dead bothered him. He knew it was risky driving through town like that, all covered up in Danny Ray's blood, but with that mess up those stairs, well, he just had to go. Now. He asked Candace is there was anything there that she'd like to have. She looked around the dark house for a minute, wiping the sweat from her neck and between her breasts. In a tired voice she said no, nothing there belonged to her. She'd gotten her due in the divorce.

When they got to the kitchen, near the back of the house, he was glad there wasn't a dog to feed. His hand was on the knob and there came a sigh of relief. He was almost done.

Candace pushed the door open and there was no breeze, no rush of warm air. The night was as flat and still as when they first pulled up. Walking out of doors, even after such a thing as committing a murder, seemed anticlimactic.

Christ, he'd have hoped for a clap of thunder or some dry lightning.

Halfway out the door when all of a sudden Candace wondered out loud where Julianne, Danny Ray's second wife was.

Well, there you go.

He was to know could she be mistaken, maybe Danny Ray hadn't married again after all. But Candace shook her head and said, yeah, far as she knew he had married a girl named Julianne.

The closet. Under the bed. Out the front door. Anywhere.

It was agonizing; one foot in and one out. Candace tugging him along and the need to wrap things up pushing him back in. He knew that if that girl was hiding somewhere, if she was back there
in that goddamned house
he had to go find her, he had to get her
Fucking Jesus Christ!
but Candace didn't want him to. She wanted to let Julianne be, leave her be wherever she was, might not be in the house at all. He knew it wasn't as simple as all that. A dog howled from somewhere in the neighborhood and Candace yanked on him again, pulling him along with her, toward the rest of the trip and even beyond. But there was still stuff to do, and the night was far from over. He imagined Julianne crouched under the bed, dialing 911 and watching the blood drip from up top the mattress and down onto the carpeting. It would never come out. That's how his one shirt was ruined.

There'd be nothing getting done long as Candace was there. There was no way he'd be up for anything else with her watching, and she'd already said she didn't want him stirring things up anymore. The only thing left to do was to rid of Candace. Send her on back to the motel and meet up with her later, just get her the hell out of there and stop making such a fucking spectacle of themselves. Something he should have done right off.

He told her go on and then guided her on ahead through Danny Ray's dog run. It was about twenty feet in length and two feet wide and ran between Danny Ray's garage and his neighbors'. It was all cluttered with junk–car parts, old dead brush that'd been cleaned up sometime last year, and the bristly skeleton of what used to be a pink-flocked Christmas tree.

They squeezed through slowly, carefully picking their way along the crowded pathway and being careful not to cut themselves on any of that old rusted metal. There were bugs too, and rats, at least field mice.

He was trying to hurry her up, get her in that car and outta there so he could sneak back in and find out what became of the second wife. But he needn't have thought so hard, because as soon as they rounded the corner of the garage and stepped into the alleyway where the Maverick was still parked, the mystery of Julianne was solved.

She greeted them head-on, bumped right into Candace and then dropped her purse, and when she bent over to pick it up he jerked his leg upward and slammed his knee into her face.

It hurt like that. He clipped it right where he was so badly bruised from falling off the bed, now he was sure he'd cut himself on Julianne's teeth. He could feel the warm, wet liquid smearing over his knees and messing up the inside of his pantleg. And it popped again too.

Candace whistled at the close call.

She wanted to know did Julianne see their faces?

He thought that she didn't. It happened too fast; all she saw was the asphalt coming her way.

She wanted to know did he kill her?

He thought no, just knocked her out.

She was a little angry that an innocent bystander—those were her words—had been hurt, and the sheer stupidity of such an idea pissed him off. He wanted to say so, but didn't. He put it off to the heat and let it go. Anyways, hadn't she been waiting on him upstairs, knowing what he was doing and all? A lot of girls would have left him high and dry. Not her.

Julianne was out cold, laying all crooked and funny-looking across the asphalt in the alleyway, her arms and legs splayed to the side and a pretty nice bruise already forming on the tip of her chin. She was a pretty girl, he noticed right away, but she was no Candace.

He reached down and snatched Julianne's bag just before they left. He knew how Candace felt about taking things that didn't belong to them—she scowled and made a loud, annoying click of disapproval with her tongue—but he thought it would look more like a robbery if something were missing. Candace went on ahead shaking her head and making noises.

She was in the car already, praying to that plastic doll again when he got in. He turned the key halfway and then waited for her to be done. It was foolish, they should've been long gone by now, but those prayers of hers seemed awfully damned important and for all he knew, they were the things that were guiding him all along.

"...assist me in this my necessity..."

He didn't know much about religion, but he wondered if it was only Catholics who prayed for God to crush their enemies and keep them safe.

He knew when she made the sign of the cross

over her chest that she was finished. She kissed the tip of her forefinger, then touched it to the head of the Blessed Virgin Mary on the dash.

"You'll keep me safe?"

Her expression soured right away upon catching sight of Julianne's bag. He had set it on the seat between the two of them but she scooted further away, as if just the touch of that item would implicate her in the theft. Her legs crossed tightly and her face all scrunched up, she refused to look his way, absolutely refused to make this long murderous night any easier on him even in the smallest way.

This too would pass, and he was conscious of the effort inside himself to not let this one thing spoil the rest of the night.

As he pulled out of the narrow alleyway and onto the cross street that would lead them back to room number 11, he began to feel a morbid sense of accomplishment, and with that, a lessening of the tightness in his chest and temples. With each block of Georgia suburb that old Maverick ate up, he felt farther from the deed and further from the danger. He was starting to feel okay, despite the blood he was smeared with from head to toe.

Just as the car hit forty, though, the giddy freedom he'd been working on turned to terror. He began to sweat and shake, just like last time after they left Bobby Lee's house. Only it was worse this time. It wasn't guilt, there hadn't been time yet for that to settle in. Maybe it was Candace. Having her. For real. Or maybe never. Maybe it was the challenge. Maybe it was the heat.

Just like earlier, when he almost pasted the two

of them to that 18-wheeler's front grill.

It was only after, when he realized what he could have lost and how close he really came.

He pulled over a few blocks from Danny Ray's house. Pulled the car over and threw up on the side of the road.

chapter five

He arrived back at the motel room alone, having lost Candace about halfway between there and Danny Ray's. She all of a sudden hollered stop the car how could you do that and all sorts of other hateful cursing and then demanded that he pull over, which he did right away. He watched her run down the side of the road like a crazy woman, her silhouette getting blacker and smaller the further she got away from him, but he let her go. He knew she'd be back. She left the dog, her makeup case, and him behind. They were all she had.

It was nearly two-thirty when he found himself at the threshold of room number 11, with nothing to show for his efforts but caked blood under his fingernails and clothes that would have to be burned. When he turned the key and kicked the door open, he was immediately struck in the face by an unbearable blast of heat mixed with the putrid stink of fresh dog pee. The mangy perpetrator was nowhere to be seen, having already ducked under one of the two twin-sized beds for cover. It was a combination that should have made him sick, but it was nothing compared to what he'd just come from.

He entered the darkened room, closed the door behind, and let the wide array of offensive smells catch in his throat. It smelled pretty bad in there, but it was mostly the heat that was hard to take.

There was an air conditioner, though it was old and rotten-looking and beaten up pretty badly. All the metal parts were laced with rust, and brown water dripped onto the rug just beneath, where it collected in a wet, spongy pile. Push buttons, black with grease and dirt from prior guests, lined the top half, and the plastic vents were all chipped and broken off, so that when he turned it on, it blew wild gusts of warm, stale air randomly through the room. He kicked it once and it wheezed; the temperature dropped slightly but he knew it wouldn't last.

Exactly when Candace would be coming home was a mystery and so he didn't want to fall asleep for fear of missing her return. He killed time, just like before, wandering the empty dark rooms and waiting on that woman.

Just above the air conditioner, next to the framed list of House Rules, was a wall radio that also appeared to be out of order. It was filthy and there were several small punctures in the gold mesh speaker cover. Using his thumbnail, he was able to turn the piece where the left knob should have been. It went 90 degrees and then there was a loud click and then, the staccato bursts of static that heightened and then died as he twirled the right knob, which was still in place, back and forth.

The music started softly and then grew louder as the radio warmed up and with some fine-tuning he had Loretta Lynn on in almost no time at all. The speaker was shot to hell and it sounded like shit, worse than the radio in the Maverick, but even in the disjointed way it sang to him there was something soothing. Alone in the dark, listening to cowgirls crooning about love gone bad, it was like coming home. The Country Western station was the only one it would pick up. He was glad; he'd had a bellyful of Paul Anka on the way up from Gainesville and didn't think he could take much more. So he listened to that. It was nice. Not as nice as the jukebox back at the Hi-N-Dri, but nice just the same.

He sat on the edge of the bed, the one with the awful floral print bedspread, and wanted to cry but hadn't the strength, so he just lay back, boots and all, and shut his eyes to the day. He tried to imagine just one part of his body that didn't ache from something.

Hardly worth thirty-five dollars a night, 'specially with her not even here.

Just on the cusp of consciousness, where the events of the day could have easily been mistaken for a wild, whiskey-induced nightmare, he began to feel safe. He relaxed the muscles in his shoulders and let himself sink deeper into the sagging mattress, lulled into a mild stupor by the constant, droning hum of the air conditioner and the twanging love songs that played in the wall.

There was just him and the heat. It occurred to him that maybe Jesus was in that room as well, or maybe, on account of it being so hot in there, it was the Devil who sat up with him. He wondered how it was that someone like Candace could be so sure she was not alone when there was never no outwardly sign that she wasn't.

His thoughts, as always, were with Candace. His mind went back to the first night, watching her and wondering what she was about and where had she come from. Some forty-eight hours later and it was he who lay in the dark wondering when the bad news would come about her being out there somewhere at four a.m.

If he'd had to lay odds on where she might be at such an hour in such a state, he would have put at least a twenty on the cops. A smart man would've been halfways to Los Angeles by now, but then again, a smart man might not have let her go. Or might not have come at all. It was hard to say, even in hindsight.

His eyes fluttered once or twice, like they do just before you drop off to sleep. He exhaled deeply, as if this cleansing breath could purge his soul of the guilt that had been dogging him in the last hour or so. In a matter of seconds, unconsciousness came like absolution. But the guilt would just follow him there. He should have seen it coming.

Of course, the dream began instantly. At precisely the moment of surrender, the moment that should have been release but never was, he felt the familiar dread of remorse and shame and even more than that, the embarrassing condemnation that he had fucked himself but good.

His sobs woke him just as quickly, and for an instant he dangled between his dream world and hell, both of which had been specifically designed to accommodate his own personal bogeyman.

Room for one more...

He jerked his body rudely out of sleep and twitched in defense. The song on the radio wasn't even over yet, he'd been asleep for fifteen seconds, maybe twenty.

A car passed on the highway, sending a flash of bright, white light streaking across the walls and the floor and then disappearing out the window, leaving just as suddenly as it had arrived. In that second, he'd seen things. He'd seen the stains on his flesh and the crimson gunk that was already set into the minute grooves of his calloused hands. He'd seen the Deed, large as life, just like when Candace flicked that light on and yanked him out of the cover of darkness and made him look at the wrath he had wrought upon her ex-husband. The sight was still there, right there in his brain where he couldn't shake it to save his soul, if indeed that's what he was intending on doing that night.

He lay flat on the bed, his arms extended straight out from his body and his hands reaching across the polyblend comforter. His legs straightened, knees knocked and feet together, and he closed his eyes, waiting for what? The hand of God.

He imagined our Lord peering down at him from inside of some cloud and he would say how long you been standing there? Again, it was hard to breath so he stopped trying. He held it in and listened for the steady, soothing hiss of Danny Ray sleeping in the dark, but there was nothing. Just an occasional whimper from underneath the bed.

Voices were there, in the dark with him. Or were they next door in number 12? He heard one, first, softly, like someone calling to him from across a field. He picked up the rhythm of the words but not what they were saying, not at first. He recoiled from the darkness and pinned himself tighter against the

Collecting Candace

mattress, palms down now, toes flexed, but it didn't stop the voice. It grew louder. It said the same thing over and over again, and he listened to one syllable at a time till finally he was able to string them all together and they came crashing toward the front of his brain, pushing out all his feelings and just stomping the shit out of all his other thoughts.

I killed a man.

Hardly seemed possible.

Two men!

And Lord, if that weren't enough to push him right over the edge, the reminder that she was not there with him was plenty.

Here lay a gentle, passive man, at least for most of his life. He loses his temper just twice in the last ten years and both times come in this one night. The first at least had purpose, the second, here and now in the motel room, was nothing more than a release of excess energy. Pent up frustration and anger and the bitter, pained realization that no, he did not forgive her for not being there.

He hurled himself up off the bed and strode to the mirror above the dresser. The muddy outline of his shadow in the glass peered back at him. It was time.

Look yourself right in the eye you bugger

but it was too dark in that cramped, stuffy room

Where is she?

to see anything but dark where his face should have been

and tell me what you see you motherfucking murdering son of a bitch so he balled up one fist and slammed it into his own reflection, spraying the room with chards of splintered glass and more blood. His open cuts burned with pain, even the warm flow of blood over the wounds didn't ease the stinging when the slivers of glass imbedded themselves into his skin, but he paid it no mind. He threw another punch, this time with the other hand, and barely winced when his knuckles broke right through the mirror and into the thin plasterboard behind. Back and forth, left, right, left, right, he pummeled the wall with his bony hand, throwing punches and throwing his weight into his anger with bloody knuckles till he'd torn huge, gaping holes in both the wall and his flesh.

Still, it was not enough. It didn't work.

He closed his eyes and felt her—not Candace, another, her hands on his chest, pushing him back, pushing him out the door and locking it tight before he could shove his way back in.

My fucking house.

He felt her kicks and heard her screams and that slap... he could hear her saying fuck you fuck off and he could see her slamming the door and leaving all her shit behind. Like he'd want it anyways.

It was Sunday. Second Sunday.

He choked on the second tears that had come to him tonight and dropped to his knees at the altar of Candace's belongings, where she had laid all her stuff out before she went out with him. One arm motioned half-heartedly to sweep them off, but instead he just threw himself over the bureau and embraced them, the perfume, the makeup and lipstick and the pieces of jewelry that she decided not to wear today.

Photos of other kids, letters to other women. Buying Jack Daniels at ten in the morning and taking a note from Mom that says it's okay and Danny Ray's gonna git you if you don't watch out and that was my favorite shirt goddamit!

He reached for the half-empty bottle of whiskey and gulped some down, not even mindful of the excess washing down his chin and neck and soaking the crewneck collar of his stained T-shirt.

Pain.

In his knees. In his balls. In his brain. He'd known her only forty-eight hours and already she'd colored him in the way that only a woman bringing destruction can.

Heaven was waiting. She'd told him so. He believed her. She'd told him there was room for everyone, that it was big as all outdoors. He took another drink and stood again, grasping the bottle in one hand and perching his other on the edge of the bureau to hold himself steady. His reflection was gone. Even the black shadow was not there. Only holes in the wall. Only blood. And a big mess.

Swiftly, decisively, he smashed the whiskey bottle on the laminated wood surface of the bureau and closed his eyes as the liquor sprayed his face and the rest of the room. The dog began to cry and he could hear a steady stream of piss under the bed. Or was it inside of his pants leg?

He had lost all feeling in his body, he was coated with liquor, blood, and the sweat that was now covering his skin in a thick, greasy layer. Every vein was swollen and bloated with liquor and every pore jammed with grime and blood from Danny Ray's open wounds.

And them came a fear, so thorough and so unforgiving, racing to his soul. Afraid to turn around, afraid to stand still, every car that hummed past on the highway was THEM. Coming for him. Every sound in that coffin of a motel room was Danny Ray, dragging his beaten, battered carcass all the way across town to look him in the eye and say what the fuck?

He had acted in righteousness and was now suffering in total repentance. Lot of good it did. He'd always suspected as much about religion.

And there was the dream. Bits of it were coming again, only this time he was awake. The dread and fear. The absolute desperation that before had haunted only his sleep was now dragging its long, scraggly fingers over the door, rooting at the stoop and sniffing for him and wanting to be let in. Like some hairy beast that comes for you in the middle of the night. Like the creatures that hide under your bed and wait for the night to come and drink your blood.

I am fucked

Figuratively, of course...

He wished some more for Candace. For her to pray with him, to pray for him.

And Patsy Cline sang sadly, soulfully on this, his dark night of the soul.

Death stalked him in that cramped, hot room. He crouched in front of the bare wall where the mirror used to be, shifting his weight clumsily from one foot to the other, and then back again, wielding the broken bottle like a weapon and fending off his own demise for as long as he could. He breathed through his mouth for fear of that smell–the smell of death–invading his nostrils, but he breathed too fast and started to hyperventilate. He was weak, he was tired, and his reflexes had been dulled by two solid days of frustration.

Recoiling from a noise in the blackness, he swaggered back and his right foot caught on the overnight bag that she had tucked halfway under her bed. He yelled out as he lost his footing and went crashing to the floor, fully expecting to disappear into a giant crack in the earth, and so relieved to fall into the narrow space between the beds. The ground was hard and that nappy carpet skinned his elbows as he floundered on the floor and tried to set himself right. The bottle had disappeared, having been flung out of reach somewheres under the other bed, and when he grabbed for it, he found instead that damned case, the contents of which had spilled out all around him.

The first thing he came upon was the only thing he needed.

The dirty blouse that she was wearing in the Hi-N-Dri, all damp and stink-filled.

He seized it like sacrament, grasping it in his hands and raising it to his tear-stained face. He rolled onto his back, fondling the filthy fabric, and draped it neatly over his face, letting the scent of her sweat and perfume overwhelm him. The thin, soiled material covered his nose and mouth so all he could taste was her. And it was good.

And God saw that it was good...

He wept.

The smell of death wafted over him like the sweetest perfume and he wept some more. He parted his lips and the tip of his tongue slipped out and he came dangerously close to tasting her flesh.

Tragedy was playing through the wall speaker and he pressed the blouse down tighter onto his face with one hand, trying to remember every prayer he'd ever heard

God is great, God is good...

and bartering his undying faith for the promise that he might live through this one night, this last night, of deliciously carnal decadence and total moral bankruptcy.

He damned near writhed in repentance on the nappy carpet, pressing her blouse tighter to his face and letting his other hand slide down the blood-stained shirt to reach for his jeans. His fingers were sore when they flexed over the damp denim, but he ignored the pain of his open wounds. In his mind, his touch grazed the smooth skin of her body and so he anxiously spread his fingers wider, just to feel her, just loving the feel of her. He gasped and flexed his fingers again, the skin split on his knuckles and he felt the blood trickling out over his groin but he didn't care. He imagined himself on the softly sloping curve of her back as it led down into the waistband of the baggy jeans.

Light from a passing big rig streamed in and slid across the floor, just like the sunlight did that first morning he met her. It wasn't her. He cried hard, the way he'd been wanting to since he met her. Wanting her so bad. Needing her. He relaxed his grip and

Collecting Candace

slowly let it in, undoing his belt buckle and the snaps of his blue jeans and pushing away the wet, slick fabric.

Oh, Lord, oh, Lord, stay with me tonight....

His head turned and he licked his lips and imagined them landing on her shoulder, where he'd suck on her lightly, right through the thin white cotton shirt he'd given her. He could taste the salt, he wanted to lick the thin layer of sweat off her entire body.

The music was getting faster and the air conditioner was dying, but not so's he'd notice.

He pushed the material between his lips and groaned. In his dreams, his lips found their way over to her bare neck, the skin was damp and cool there in the hollow of her throat when he kissed her. His hands were slick; it could have been sweat or blood, either way, it felt good.

Thoughts of the dead man and the dead man's wife tried to crowd his brain but the feel of Candace, real or otherwise, pushed them right out again.

He groaned in surrender and rolled over onto one side, drawing his knees to his chest and curling himself up in a tight ball. One hand clutched her blouse to his face, the other pushed furiously between his legs.

His prayers had not been answered.

There'd be no sleeping in there tonight.

chapter six

Jesus left before dawn, having been summoned under false pretenses in the first place.

"Would you still love me if I was bad?"

His eyes fluttered but did not open.

What the fuck?

He lay flat on his back, his shoulders pinned to the rough carpet and his swollen, aching body unable to pull them off. His tongue was fat and dry; he ran it over his gritty teeth just once and then reached blindly for the bottle that he'd forgotten had been broken last night.

"Would you still love me if I was bad?"

His mind raced, as fast as was able for it being so early and for him being in such a state, for clues that might answer this perplexing question which she had already asked him twice. He could think of nothing that was said or done yesterday to foretell the best response, so he lay still and kept his eyes closed, feigning sleep and trying to get his bearings on this, yet another strange new day.

The air conditioner hummed in futility from somewhere on the other side of the room. It was the last sound he'd heard last night before passing out and it had soothed him in his solitude then, but its faint gasp was of little comfort in the light of day. He managed to open one eye, but the sun coming between the mesh in the curtains was too bright and he squeezed it shut again immediately. Seconds later, on the count of three, he opened both of them and looked down the length of his raggedy, worn body. He still lay on the floor between the beds, neither of which had been slept in.

Is this about that goddamned Virgin Mary thing? Is that what this is about?

He was still dressed in the clothes he wore the night before, but they smelled much worse. His jeans were damp with sweat, blood, and more and during the night the wet parts had hardened so that the slightest movement would now produce an awful chafing in his groin. He shifted his weight over to his right hip and winced at the way his Levis scraped the delicate skin between his thighs. He'd have liked to cut those pants right off his body, right where he lay.

His T-shirt, which used to be white, was stained all over with different shades of red, some in washed-out streaks of magenta, like watercolors, some in hard, darkened, crusted puddles, the combination of which made it look like somebody had vomited their guts all over his chest. In some places, where the heat had not yet dried the blood, the material stuck like adhesive to his body and the viscous red stuff soaked into his bare flesh underneath. His hard, flat belly was exposed where the T-shirt had been pushed out of the way last night. He had been stained there too, and the curly black hairs just below his navel were matted with blood and salty, crusted puddles of se-men.

He groaned, and she put it to him once more.

"Would you still love me if I was bad? I must know."

Jesus was surely gone from this place today. But Candace was back.

He told her yes and that seemed to suit her.

She sat contentedly near his feet, humming to herself and gathering up the bits of her life that had fallen from the suitcase in her absence. She noticed him watching her and she smiled. She motioned with her head at the room, which lay in ruin all around them.

"You miss me?"

He nodded.

She gazed at the mess at her feet. "Looks like it."

He nodded again and then she smiled once more, innocently and lewdly both at once, as she reached up between his thighs and snatched the dirty blouse that he held in his hand.

"You don't want this ratty old thing."

He reluctantly let it slip between his bruised, swollen fingers, now caked with fresh, bloodied scabs, and struggled to raise himself up on his elbows, but they too were raw and skinned and he could feel one of the cuts open fresh all over again. He heaved himself up into a sitting position and pulled his starched T-shirt away from his chest, but it was like cardboard. It stank to high heaven, made him want to retch, but Candace didn't seem to even notice.

God bless her.

Covered from head to toe in some man's blood, hell, in her husband's blood, and she sat there like she didn't see nothin' and like she couldn't taste it thick in the air when she breathed through her mouth. But he could.

He pushed his palm back over his hair, which was also matted with grease and with blood, and smiled at her, a little embarrassed for looking like such shit, but happy to see her there just the same.

The sight of her immediately extinguished last night's radical thoughts of regret. Remorse still hung in the air, though, along with the stink of pee and liquor, but a hot shower, something to eat, and an open window would soon fix all that.

There was much to talk about, but even after a full thirty seconds of staring one another down, nothing came. The silence was long but not awkward, and after another minute or so of it, they decided there wasn't that much to say after all. He figured that she left because she just needed some time, he guessed that what had happened yesterday was, after all, a gruesome thing to behold. And he hoped that she wouldn't read too much into the sight that lay before her when she let herself in with the key this morning. He needn't have worried.

Candace went about her housework. She sorted some old postcards and letters that lsy askew from when he kicked them aside last night.

"Lookit." She smiled and offered him a dog-eared black-and-white photo. A man and a child, he guessed it was her father and there was no doubt it was her. They sat languidly on that same front porch he had visited, the family of squirrels not yet in attendance, eyeing the camera with indifference. She was about nine and was posed in her old man's lap, her right arm slung casually around his neck, her left dangling off behind. She looked very young and carefree in a little flowered sundress; the stern-looking black shoes and plain anklets seemed out of character, though, like an outfit a father would choose.

The man held her tightly and was smiling broadly but crookedly. His left arm was draped around behind her, his hand flattened into the small of her waist, holding on tight so she wouldn't slip off his knee and down off the back of the chair. His right hand was tucked neatly between her legs, his palm cupping her bare knee and his thumb just peeking under the fold of her hem.

She eyed him anxiously while he studied the photo, biting her lip in the most awfully cute way and nibbling on her thumbnail. She was waiting for it, to hear it or at the very least to see it in his eyes. Her guilty conscience loomed over them in the most gaudy, obvious way and still she clung to subtlety. She wanted to know if he could see it. If it was there in the picture and if the whole world knew too or was it just her shame?

He choked back the gagging reflex and resisted the urge to shred that fucking photo into a million pieces. Instead, he smiled and remarked that she looked very pretty and he'd wished he'd known her then and she seemed relieved that was all that was said.

The photo dropped to the floor and he pushed up off the ground, stepping carefully over the blades of glass that littered the rug, even though he still wore his boots.

Collecting Candace

He moved away, stretching his legs and trying to pop his knees back into place, and all he could think about was the bruise on her back and the way she cried last night. He thought of the way that slap had sounded out there in the middle of nowhere and of the strange silent man who cowered behind a painted screen door and watched his daughter run off in the middle of the night with some other man.

A picture surely is worth a thousand words.

There was much to do today but suddenly all he wanted to do was go back and visit Candace's dad, but there was plenty of time for that.

None of his other chores seemed worth pulling himself out of that room where she still sat on the floor, cross-legged and cute as a fucking bug.

Still ignorant of the mess that lay around her, she sorted out the rest of her belongings before stuffing them back into her overnight bag. There were some fresh panties–Sunday, Wednesday, and Friday all spelled in different shades of embroidery thread–a couple of dresses, a box of tampons and a half-eaten chocolate bar that had gone soft from the heat. Buried underneath the rubble was a gold chain she picked carefully from the carpet and held up to the light. It was strung with three small wedding bands and a Saint Christopher medal, and this she put around her neck while he padded off to the bathroom for a shower.

When he emerged thirty minutes later, his skin scrubbed raw and the stink of Danny Ray removed from his person, he found a hearty breakfast of bacon and eggs that she had gone out and bought at the diner a couple of blocks away.

She was on the phone when he came out of the john, her back turned to him so that she didn't see him enter the room. She mumbled in that faint, conspiratorial way, and though he tried to shrug it off, he couldn't help but hang back a safe enough distance just to hear who she might be talking to. No matter how hard he tried to think otherwise, the sight of her talking on that telephone was, for him, the Judas kiss all over again.

It would have been easy to kill her, but he knew he'd have to follow. So instead, he came up behind her and rested his palms on her hips and kissed her bare shoulder, once.

She squealed and turned around quick and giggled, placing the phone back on the receiver. She nuzzled up to him, rubbing her cheek against his, freshly shaved and smelling of mint, but he pulled away. He wanted to know who was that on the phone and after a minute of not wanting to tell she said her dad.

She kissed him again and he had to believe her. Had to. No choice.

"Time to eat," she said as she took his hand and led him back to the table where his breakfast was cooling fast.

She had spread out his meal on the little table next to the television, had propped open the square Styrofoam container and laid his plastic fork and knife on the napkin. A cup of tepid coffee sat on the right, and she giggled with pride as she sat across from him and watched him eat.

Though it was hot in the room, the air wasn't nearly as suffocating as it had been the night before.

Collecting Candace

It smelled like pine, hot pine, and he noticed the bottle of cleaner that sat up top the bureau. She'd opened a couple of windows and turned the air conditioner on high, hoping to flush out the pungent aromas that had soaked into the carpet and drapes and he could see where the carpet was wet from her trying to scrub up the stains, but mostly they were still there. The dog was gone, she'd tied him up just outside the door so that he could get some fresh air and so that they might be alone for a little while.

He wondered what time it was as he shoveled a heaping forkful of scrambled eggs into his mouth and washed it down with cold coffee. Anywhere else they would have tasted like shit and he'd have given them to the dog, but this morning in Decatur they were just right.

The drapes held off very little of the light, and for the first time he got a good look at the damage he'd done the night before. Though most everything was back in its place and though she had worked hard to set everything right, the room had clearly seen a bad night. The liquor had all been wiped off the bureau, she'd found the broken bottle and it now lay upside down in the small plastic wastebasket, its jagged edges sticking straight up and out. His dirty clothes had been stuffed into a garbage bag and placed by the front door. The only true reminder of his dismal evening without her came from the icicles of shattered glass that still littered the carpet. Those, and the wall where the mirror used to hang. It was now bare and pockmarked with chipped-out of plaster and thick, red streaks like snot that trailed off into nothing as they were wiped over the wall.

He downed another mouthful of eggs and with his right hand adjusted the white towel that was draped around his hips. The vinyl seat stuck to his bare ass where the material was riding up in the back, and he suddenly became self-conscious in front of her. She only blushed, as if she could read his thoughts.

Two down, and one to go. This close. This fucking close.

He wanted to hear now about Joe, Just Plain Joe, but she only shook her head and looked away, remarking awkwardly about what a mess the room was in and was the manager going to charge them extra.

And then without saying a word and meaning to change the subject, she got up and retrieved a stack of cards from her tote bag. He thought they looked like Bicycle playing cards but they weren't. They were prayer cards. All slick and laminated and very professional-looking. He pressed his forefinger to one that lay close by and he slid it over to his side of the table. On one side was a picture of Jesus. On the other, The Lord's Prayer written neatly in calligraphy.

Our Father, who art in heaven,

Like the baseball cards he and his old man had collected when he was just six or seven. He wondered whatever became of Mickey Mantle and wondered if those might be waiting for him in The Box, back in Gainesville.

She fingered the stack of them, shuffling them like a hustler and flipping them over onto the table in front of her. He wondered was she gonna tell his fortune and if she was he might just say don't bother with it.

He remarked how if a girl were going to pack for a trip away with a man, that those cards might be a strange choice but her face clouded over and she thought maybe not so strange, but she wouldn't elaborate.

He grunted and wanted to know what prayers got her anyway, and she just smiled and said well they got me you, didn't they, and he said he'd never thought of it like that before.

She laid them all across the table, face up, and admired their painted faces under the slippery plastic covers. She touched her fingertips to each one, reading them, like one of those tarot readers, and he got a chill down his back and decided not to ask her what she was praying for now. He was scared to know 'cause, so far, all her prayers were coming true.

He felt the vinyl sweating under his bare skin and adjusted himself so, but it hurt when he touched the rash between his legs. Watching her there, even holding those prayer cards, yeah, he wanted to fuck her and he worried that it was against heaven or some such shit. He was too sore anyways from all that dry humping and dreaming about her all night.

He shifted in his seat and asked about Joe again and this time it made her get up and turn her back to him. He wanted to know what the big deal was and why she couldn't talk about it but she just shrugged her shoulders.

"Nothin' to tell, I guess," she sighed.

Joe was her first, that much he knew. First lay, first husband, first loss, everything she was all balled up into one man who was God knew where right at this moment. The other two, they were deserving bastards when they'd died, but Joe seemed to merit none of the ill-will that she wistfully spoke of during conversations about the others. If murder could be easy, well, then Bobby Lee and Danny Ray certainly could make it so. There didn't have to be motive, nor just cause: they needed it. Pure and simple. They needed it.

But Joe was gonna be trouble. Dead or alive, in Gainesville or out, he was still sitting right there in the catbird seat, right there in the back of Candace's mind. Big as life, no, bigger, and there seemed no way to touch him.

She'd easily 'fessed up about the others, she'd eagerly confided her worst nightmares in regards to husbands number two and three, and that made her stubbornness regarding Joe that much more confusing. She'd led him right to the others, led the way on this quest, but this time seemed almost to protect these cherished, virgin memories of Just Plain Joe. Hard as it was to believe, that's what she seemed to be doing and it was pissing him off plenty.

He wanted to ask if Joe was so fucking wonderful then how come he was gone but he didn't, for he knew that was surely a question to get him slapped.

Instead, he tossed his meal into the trash and went to help her pick the glass up off of the carpeting.

He wanted to know wasn't there one goddamned thing this guy did that she was mad at.

"Oh, sure," she said, as if stating the obvious. "He left me." She sighed as she gingerly picked a small sliver of shattered mirror from underneath the bureau.

Fucking bastard...

He crouched beside her, taking care not to step on any of the glass, and sighed, looking at her sideways as she concentrated on the task at hand.

"There's a Bar-B-Q place somewhere out here," she said, without looking up from the carpet. "It's got great food, I'm gonna take you there, when we leave, on the way out of town."

He nodded and smiled sweetly at her and she continued, excited by his gentle encouragement.

"They've got the best Bar-B-Q you've ever tasted, I guarantee that, and cold beer too... and it's cheap," she added as she tilted her palm over the wastebasket and let a shower of glass sprinkle the inside. "Now, where was it...let me think...I only seen it once but it's around here somewhere..."

She became pensive, thinking out loud about directions and where to turn and was it east or west and Jesus, it had been so long since Danny Ray had taken her out there. He only half listened as she cursed her poor memory, couldn't even remember the name of the place.

"...Now where the hell..." Her voice trailed off as she fixed her eyes on a small piece of glass imbedded in the short pile carpeting. He winced, watching her use her thumbnail to try and dig it out while getting angrier and angrier about that place with the good Bar-B-Q.

"It's... just out of town... ugh... it's... oh, hell..." She pushed her long blond hair out of her face and gently chewed on her lower lip and it was plain she was getting plenty mad all over again. He remembered the last time she got all mad and he knew what that spelled for him and it was bad.

"I'll have to ask...oh, Christ..." She let out an exasperated sigh, as you would at just having remembered something unpleasant, and he became self-conscious again. She fell back onto her rear and stared at that little piece of glass and looked like she was about to cry. "We'll just have to forget it, I guess..." she said sullenly and then slapped her ankle for emphasis. "...well, fuck!"

Her lip trembled and her eyelids drooped and he reached out to touch his thumb to her cheek in a loving gesture but she slapped his hand away angrily.

"Fuck you," she growled.

He touched her anyway and she slapped him again, this time harder, not fucking around. Before he could react, she slapped his wrist too, and then his forearm and now she was starting to cry and flail her hands at him in a fury. He tried to grab hold of her wrists but she squirreled away and clipped him once across the face and got him in probably the only part of his whole body that didn't hurt yet from something.

Her anger took him completely by surprise. Her confusion and angst he had been living with and, he thought, taking care of. But her anger, hatred-like in its intensity, frightened him.

He turned for her, tried to open his arms and pull her in and hold her tight, stroke her hair and whisper in her ear and make it okay, but she began to fight and claw and gasp in resistance. Every slap of her palm and every dig of her nails sent a reeling pain through some cut-up part of his body. She jerked with wrath as he wrapped himself around her and her fingers found their way to his cheeks, where she howled and dug her nails into the soft flesh.

"God, oh, God, oh, God, oh, God! What did you do? What did you do to me?" She slapped her palms to his face in a pounding, relentless rhythm, punctuating her sorrow with wails of grief.

He tried to tell her just what it was that he'd done for her and he tried to make her see but he knew that if she didn't get it now and if she were allowed to leave his embrace then he'd never get her back.

She only cried more and shook all over with heaving, desperate sobs and could only repeat I'm afraid I'm afraid over and over and over again till the words ran together and made no sense at all to him.

He was going to protect her and he told her so. He was going to keep her safe and make it alright for her again and he reminded her about how it was going to be, about how it had to be, but she just cried harder and buried her face in his neck where her salty tears stung his cuts.

Her fingers clawed at his back and she pushed herself into his bare chest and grabbed onto him tight and soon she was pulling him closer, pulling him in and wrapping his body around hers as tight as it would go. And she would not stop crying.

Pray with me, pray with me now...

"Help me!" she howled and thrust herself into his chest again. "Help me..."

He pushed her back and grabbed her face with his hands and then brought her in close again. She was slick with tears but he kissed her hard anyway, pressing his cut lips to hers and smearing himself good and thick with her tears and her saliva.

She sobbed and dragged her lips over his, whispering to him between gasps for air. "They're gone... oh, God..." She started to whimper again. "They're gone... gone..."

They're gone!

"Gone, gone, all gone," she chanted over and over until she had no strength left. His lips were pressed against her wet cheek and he was trying to shush her and it seemed like hours since she's broken down but it was only a couple of minutes that he held her so tight.

She whimpered with one last gust of energy and slapped him again but he ignored it and gradually, her sobs subsided and she curled up against his chest, trembling and shaking and unable to think at all. He could feel her body collapse into his and he felt good. Proud. He'd been there for her, not like the others, and that's all she must remember.

They sat together on the stained carpet for another ten minutes or so, just stroking and breathing and trying not to start crying again. She was a sorry-looking thing but he loved her like the devil.

It was quiet again in the motel room, except for the wheezing air conditioner that was now blowing hot, wet air into their eyes.

And then he did a stupid thing.

He reached over and pinched that piece of glass between his thumb and forefinger, the one she was fighting with when things went bad, but it was stuck hard. He jabbed his thumbnail into the rug, like she'd done, but he used too much force and the pressure sent that little sliver of mirror right under his skin and deep into his flesh.

Jesus fucking Christ....

He yelped like a dog who'd been kicked and he jumped to his feet, jerking Candace out of her stupor and pushing her back onto the rug. The pain shot up his arm and into his brain and he shook his hand hard, like some fucking beast's jaws were dug in tight. But it didn't help, just splattered Candace's shirt with three drops of fresh, warm blood. His blood.

It looked like a small cut but it had gone deep, and he was bleeding pretty bad for it being such a little thing. The blood started to drip quickly from his finger and onto the carpet and that was absolutely the last thing they needed now, especially since she had worked so hard to get rid of all that shit from the night before. He grasped his wrist with the other hand, foolishly thinking he could stop the flow of blood, but his hand just throbbed worse than before and was really starting to fucking hurt.

That's what you get, you stupid ass, trying to do every goddamn thing for her.

That fucker was in deep, and there was nothing he could do but stand there and bleed.

Fucking might as well bleed to death.

Candace reached for him and his first instinct was to recoil in defense, but she stepped closer and held his wrist with one hand and the bleeding thumb with her other. She raised it close to her face so that she could inspect it more carefully, and they both watched it oozing blood down between his fingers, over the back of his hand and down onto the rug. He winced as she blew on it and he whimpered like a child, turning his face away so he didn't have to watch whatever surgery she was going to perform.

His whole body tensed, every muscle, every nerve, everything about him was balled up about as tight as it could go. He could have laughed, seeing himself be such a pussy when those other men, hell, they'd known real suffering and hardly made a peep. Only it wasn't funny.

He'd cut himself ten times worse last night, but that hadn't hurt like this. He hadn't felt a thing last night. Was it the liquor? The shock? Grief? Or was it just this new kind of suffering?

He could feel her coming nearer and he braced himself, digging his toes into the carpet and locking his knees so that he wouldn't pass out when the needle touched his skin. His hand, and hers, were slick with blood and perspiration; he could feel it on his belly too, dripping down onto the fresh, clean white towel he'd donned just a few minutes ago.

He squeezed him up tight some more and waited for the prick, the pain when she'd dig that fucking piece of glass out. But the pain never came. He flinched when something touched his thumb, but it wasn't the cold steel blade of a knife or a needle or anything like that. It was warm, soft, and wet. Again.

Ahhhhh...

He dropped his shoulders and relaxed his grip and cocked his head to one side, waiting for it once more.

Again.

Collecting Candace

Slick and warm and feeling so good. Not rough, like he'd expected. No pain.

He opened one eye to see her staring straight at him, just the way she'd done that one morning she woke up. Her stare was fixed tight on his and he could have fainted right over when he saw the tip of her soft, pink tongue protruding from between those lips and grazing the tip of his throbbing, bleeding thumb.

She tasted a second drop of blood and he gasped, not from pleasure but from the sight of it. He raised his hand a few inches, gently pushing it up to her lips and offering it to her willingly.

Blood of my...oh, shit

Her white skin was dotted with a small drop of blood, like a crimson birthmark, near the corner or her mouth; she licked it away quickly and hummed with contentment, her gaze still locked onto his and he felt a rush that he swore could not till that day have been felt by any man alive.

She closed her eyes and parted her lips a little more, allowing the tip of his thumb to slip in between and take refuge in the warmth of her wet, willing mouth. The pain had virtually disappeared and he felt only the gentle contractions of her sucking as she took him in deeper and wrapped her tongue around his swollen digit.

He groaned loudly and felt himself sway backward, but she grabbed his wrist tightly and moved him back into place. He could feel that fucking piece of glass, he could feel it in there but it didn't hurt anymore. It was coming, with the gentle prodding of her mouth and her tongue, the way she gingerly scraped the tip over her lower teeth, he could feel her manipulating it, manipulating him, taking care of him.

Just like she said she would.

He bent his head and closed his eyes and gave in, his hand held limply in the air, his thumb engulfed deep in her mouth. The heat was intense, the air in there was unbearable and the sweat was pouring down his back and soaking that little white towel, but it felt better than any other place, any other time, in the whole fucking world.

Her gasps were soft, her groans almost inaudible, but the sound of her lips on his skin and that gentle sucking noise that she made when his thumb slid even deeper still drove him half mad. The other half came with the rhythm of her kisses, the way his entire being was sucked in there every time she took a breath and began again.

Christ almighty...

He began to breathe heavily, erratically. He opened his eyes and watched her face as she began to pull his thumb out slowly from between her lips. It was a sight that was damn near impossible to take standing on two feet. He watched her push it out further and could feel the tip of her tongue expelling him, gently, evenly, and then, with one final thrust, pushing him out completely and leaving him dangling there in the heat, barely able to breathe and not even giving a fuck if he could or not.

Candace opened her eyes slowly and stared at him lewdly. She wore a wide, satisfied grin, and then slowly bared her teeth, and then she opened her mouth and stuck out her tongue, on which sat a small, glistening shard of mirror. She gingerly picked it off and dropped it into the wastebasket, and then licked the tip of her pinky and slid it across her lower lip, wiping up a remnant drop of his blood.

He stepped back and took a deep breath, and then turned for the bathroom to dress, leaving his stained, damp towel on the floor where it had fallen.

Candace knelt on the carpet and went back to cleaning up the glass all around her feet and when he looked back, peering at her from behind the corner, he saw his woman, and again, he felt that pride.

They spent the rest of the day in the darkened room, peeking out between the drapes every once in awhile to judge how high in the sky the sun was and checking to see that nobody'd stolen their dog. His excitement had been growing ever since that afternoon and it was getting harder and harder to sit still with her anywhere in his vicinity at all. His finger throbbed now and again from the splinter she'd taken out, but all in all was a small price to pay.

Finally, around eight-thirty he went off to the front office and paid the bill, an extra fifty dollars for the damage, and when he got back to the room Candace had already loaded up their things and piled herself and the dog into the car as well.

He gave a wink to the Blessed Virgin Mary and, feeling like a new man, barreled down the long motel drive and out onto the main drag that would lead to the interstate, and then back to Gainesville.

Home.

The night held more promise than he imagined anything ever would. With Candace by his side, and their dog in the back, and the street where Danny Ray lived—the neighborhood where that bastard with the boat lived—fading more with each passing mile marker, six hours would make all the difference in the world. Just six short hours, the time it would take to reach Gainesville if they drove straight on through, would make the difference between a criminal act and an expression of love. Between a life shrouded in guilty complicity and one resurrected by the liberating deed of murder in the first degree.

He drove slowly, keeping the car well under the speed limit, wishing there were a longer way to take so that he could make the night last a while longer, so that he could revel in the righteousness that he was loving so much. Candace sat silently beside him, would speak up occasionally to remark on something off the highway that had caught her eye, or maybe to say out loud some more of her private thoughts, but for the most part, she was still. Her fingers were tangled loosely in his, and her thumb tapping absentmindedly against his knuckles. Her other hand moved across the back of his neck in gentle, familiar strokes, her fingers tracing faint circles that grew bigger and bigger and then smaller again, tickling him so and giving him goose bumps but feeling so good that there was no way he could ask her to stop.

The dog dreamed in the backseat.

Even the weather had deigned to give its blessing upon this night. For the first time in weeks the temperature had dropped below eighty. The air was still soggy when standing still, but on the highway, going fifty-two miles an hour, a cool breeze blew through

Collecting Candace

the inside of the hatchback, making their long trip not only bearable but downright pleasant.

The road stretched out ahead, just on the other side of the snotted-up windshield. Hell, the whole world lay stretched out before them. There were very few other cars on the road; only a few times did they find themselves in sight of somebody else's brake lights, and then he would just ease up on the accelerator and widen the distance between himself and Candace and the rest of the world.

All around them was black, but once in a while, off to one side, they'd see somebody's porch light burning like a weak beacon, waiting up for someone to come home for dinner.

With all the windows rolled down, every now and then the breeze would carry in the delicious aroma of somebody's home cooking. It would linger in the car with them for a few hundred yards, and it would remind them of things, and then it would be gone.

He couldn't wait to get home and taste Candace's home cooking. Even if she couldn't cook for shit—and he was sure that she couldn't—he longed to stand in the doorway of the kitchen and see her there at the stove. He wanted to watch her from behind, watching her fussing over his dinner and stirring things in big pots. He yearned for the simple pleasure of watching her wash vegetables and splash some of that cool water over her face to refresh herself and then reach down and slip the dog a piece of raw potato before shooing him away.

He pushed his hips forward and slouched comfortably in his seat, grinning to himself and enjoying every sensation of this night. His left arm dangled outside the car door and his fingers tapped the sheet metal in time with the oldies station, which Candace was able to pick up again once they were a little ways out of town.

There had been moments—back at Danny Ray's, back at the motel—when self-recrimination loomed larger than the threat of prison and when faith strained under the weight of justice. They'd each had their moment when each struggled with their conscience, with the fear that God put into them and the fear that their mothers wished upon them, but in the end each found their only sanctuary in one another—in total surrender, utter devotion and glorious self-subjugation.

Love is a wonderful thing.

With so much behind them now, there was very little left to do for the quest to be fulfilled, and what was left would be handled the moment they arrived back in Gainesville. He wanted to get married. He wanted a wife. He wanted Candace. More than that, he yearned for her.

She was being more generous with her memories of Joe. She recalled any number of anecdotes and funny little asides from her brief first marriage, though none seemed to have the bite that he hoped they would. Most were just bland remembrances of places they had been and things they had seen, just more anonymous recollections that might have belonged to anyone.

Ironically, he'd have much rather heard that the bastard slapped her around. That he'd slept with her best friend or even fucked her mother. He'd have loved to hear how he choked a kitten or some such crime. He knew it wasn't fair to expect things to be so simple, but anyone so vile in spirit was simply waiting to die, and that's what he wanted to know more than anything: that Just Plain Joe was sitting there waiting to die, and not a soul would be surprised, nor any worse off than they were before, when he finally did.

She did repeat that Joe had left her, but this, with the passage of time, she seemed to forgive as well.

He was nervous about the last one, about Joe. Being so close to the end kept pushing his thoughts even farther beyond, toward preachers and wedding vows and wedding nights. It was hard to concentrate and to stay in that one place, with Joe, for the remainder of the time it would take. It, being the last, fueled excitement that much more.

He hoped that there wouldn't be much of a fight; he was sure he wouldn't enjoy this one any, and come to think of it, it unsettled him some that he might have enjoyed the others at all.

He snuck a sideways peek at her, her face softly lit by the dash lights and her hair blowing all around her face and in her eyes, and a giddy anticipation of their first night together, their first real night together, seized him balls first and he had to clear his throat to keep from giggling.

She smiled at him, a sexy smile that just showed the bottom of her two front teeth. She asked him what he was laughing at; he said nothing, baby, just happy is all.

Life was good.

chapter seven

It didn't last. It couldn't. And the ray of light that finally bathed them in glory

Come into the light

came not from Heaven, but from the Georgia State Police.

It came from behind. It pierced the back window of the Maverick and slammed right into the rearview mirror, where it exploded and splattered all over the inside of the car and the first sensation he was even aware of was the heat.

Jesus, it don't never let up.

Like a million watts of power all at once.

In the instant that he felt the light, the peace they had enjoyed since leaving the motel left them and there hadn't yet been time for anything to take its place. There was nothing—not panic, not even waiting for it. He experienced only the light.

Candace hissed something from her side of the car and he knew that if she were praying then she'd better fucking make it good this time.

The dog whined from the backseat, and the light got brighter still.

From the beginning, there had been fear. Even in the best of times, when she reached for his hands after the second one and when he dreamt of kissing her and holding her, the fear was still there; low lev-

els of the stuff went creeping around in the back of
his brain most all the time since they left the Hi 'n'
Dri. But it was slight and was mostly ignored except
for that one episode in the motel room, and that was
supposed to have been only temporary.

It was back now, as if that fucking light were
leaving nothing hidden, not the minute cracks in the
dash, not the angst that he'd been working on for the
past seventy-two hours, not the fear he felt since the
night before, when left alone in that fucking heat.

His mind was suddenly everywhere all at once,
but no place where it could do him any good, not
with that light in his eyes and on the back of his
neck and heating up the inside of that car by at least
twenty degrees.

There was Bobby Lee's
with blood all over the kitchen.

A red light, then a blue, sparked up behind the
Maverick. He slid forward in the seat and gripped
the steering wheel at ten o'clock and at two o'clock.
His fingers flexed and he pushed his shoulders back.
He should have been thinking about what to do
next, but all that came to him was a rehash of where
he'd been for the past three days.

There was the motel,
where such a mess was made the night before.

A siren blipped and drowned out Lesley Gore
and he remembered the smell of that home cooking
out on the highway and he wanted to just die and
thought it was funny how some things you wish for,
you get—some, you don't.

Candace's daddy, for Chrissakes...
There was all she'd said about heaven and how

it was easy enough for most folks to get in and he remembered that he never did find that broken piece of bottle that slipped out of his grasp and it was mostly stupid, useless thoughts that he was having now, instead of how far to the state line and did he have enough gas to gun the engine?

His right foot still worked, it tapped the accelerator pedal twice but the rest of his body went dead with fear.

The dog walked in small circles over the back seat and sniffed the windows.

Oh, Christ, I stole that fucking dog.

Candace was turned round backwards in her seat, shielding her eyes like it would help any and staring right into the light, but all he could do was look straight ahead at all that useless highway that was just laying there.

This was the part of the dream that he could never remember before. It was the part that he'd just as soon not.

The patrol car eased up on the left side of the Maverick, and the beam swung slightly to the right, soaking the awful brown interior of their car with the most absolute light he'd ever seen. It reflected in the windshield and flashed like a fucking A-bomb across his face and he knew they could see every move he made. With light like that, they could see every thought too and there weren't a damn thing he could do about it. His entire body–hands, legs, face–every part of him ached in anticipation of being flung from the car and thrown face-first into this long stretch of Georgia highway. He could imagine just how it would feel too, the pitted asphalt that

Collecting Candace

would scratch his chin and his elbows so bad.

The beam hit his ear and it was so hot there just like the sun. He would have traded five-to-ten for an hour of rain. The patrol car came closer and the beam crept up slowly and mixed with the red and the blue and turned the inside of that Maverick into some kind of fucking psychedelic nightmare.

Stained glass Technicolor. Even hell has it.

The siren blipped again and he let up on the accelerator, slowing easing the car over to the shoulder of the road. The gravel crunched under the tires and he could smell the heat of the engine, now that the breeze was gone.

A trail of blood half a mile wide and motive that could choke a horse.

He should have looked over, he knew that the longer it took for him to stop, the longer it took for him to look over there and smile and wave

Say, officer, I don't think I was speeding...

the worse it looked. And state police, well, they were a suspicious lot to begin with and he knew he wasn't making it any easier for himself or for Candace, especially for Candace, who was now herself square in the middle of that fucking light. He turned to see her, to see what they were looking at with that high beam; she was frozen with fear, and guilt was written all over her face

Christ, those fucking Catholics

and with a heavy heart he wondered if she would sit out in the rain at five a.m. on the side of the road and sing hymns for his soul.

This would surely mean a raise for someone back at the station.

He wished he'd fucked her just once
Christ!
when he'd had the chance.

He stared straight ahead now and braced himself for the click of a pistol in his left ear. He was motionless, and prayed for it to come quickly, before the dream got any further on and when the high beam clicked off and the interior of the car went dark again, he bit his lip to keep from crying 'cause Christ would that look bad.

His left ear itched and he wanted to scratch it bad but he was afraid to move his hands off of the steering wheel. Was afraid to turn the car off, for fear they'd think he was reaching for his gun; afraid to leave it running, in case they might think he was ready to tear outta there at any minute.

It seemed like five full minutes before his eyes could adjust to the light again, and even though it was more likely just a couple of seconds, he spent that time blind like a fucking bat, laying on the tracks and sleeping in the path of only Lord knows what.

He saw them, two of them, hard and nasty-looking and seeming like they'd just as soon shoot you dead as give you the time of day, but it could have been just his guilty conscience. They were young, maybe rookies, and he was thinking that if he'd brought even two more bullets he could get out of this one, but he was unarmed.

They just stared at him, just watched him squirm in that seat and they could probably tell he had no weapon. Lord, they were loving it, them, fingering their rifles and covering one another, and him, pee soaking his Levis and weighted down with not only a girl, but a dog as well.

He wondered if they'd gas his dog or if they'd send it back to that little blond thing that was probably missing it so bad.

"Hey, you..."

He loosened his grip on the steering wheel and pulled his foot off the accelerator and engine of the Maverick hummed in low idle. Just two feet away he could hear the rumbling of that V-8 in the patrol car and he knew he was stuck for good. The radio was still on, playing Paul Anka again,

for Chrissakes can't nothin' go right tonight?

but it was mostly drowned out by the flat, nasal commands of the dispatch operator on the two-way radio over there in the next car. In between her talking he heard loud cracks and pops. It was just like them cop shows where you go along for a real live arrest and you can hear cops fucking around on the mike and telling dirty jokes in between their bragging on catching some fucking scum.

"...I'm talking to you..."

He knew he was gonna cry but hoped that he could hold it in till he and Candace were separated. He lifted his hands slowly, palms facing forward and head facing front; more than anything he wanted to look at Candace, but knowing that she was watching this was more than he could stand.

"You listening to me, or what?"

It seemed stupid, but he hadn't expected it to end like this. He'd always imagined that he'd get to Candace before they got to him and here he was, about to be yanked out of the cover of that car, plucked from Candace's arms before knowing how the rest of it would have turned out.

He thought about the killings, starting going over them in his mind; he knew he'd be talking about them plenty in the next twenty-four hours. He didn't know if he felt remorse, but he was real sorry he'd been caught.

"You dumb asshole, look at me when I'm talking to you!"

If there was any good thing to come of this at all, he'd have to think it was that these stupid fucking state police were all but guaranteeing him martyrdom–in Candace's eyes, at least–by taking him prematurely, and it was gonna be hard now for her not to love him forever.

Hell, it was something

He could almost feel the barrel nudging his ear as he turned slowly and looked that young patrolman straight in the face.

Shoot me

His hands were almost shoulder height inside that tiny front seat of the Maverick and he knew that soon he'd be outside, hugging asphalt, spread eagle and under some lawman's knee, right there in the middle of the highway for his woman, and passers-by, to gawk at.

Let her see you do it, let it burn the memory into her brain and let her take it with her to church every fucking Sunday for the rest of her life.

He felt the tears on his cheeks and he bit his lip harder as his hands came into sight.

"Hey, asshole, your taillight's out, did you know that? You want me to write you up?"

Collecting Candace

Candace exhaled and whistled through her teeth and the dog stopped its pacing in the backseat. It whimpered once and then barked out the window, from where the light had come from and one of those cops yelled you'd better hold onto that fucking mutt I'll shoot it.

The other one laughed from the driver's side of the patrol car and said sheeeit and they pulled away before his brain could put together even a no sir.

Mel Carter came on and he broke down
when you make me tell you I love you
and then he wept for ten minutes and first he was so fucking scared and then he was so happy he couldn't stand it and every time Candace would say what's wrong baby he'd just shake his head and try and catch his breath. Pretty soon another tear would come, wetting his face and smearing him in grief.

He'd broken down and he thought he'd wet himself and all right in front of Candace but Christ that was the scariest moment he'd ever known in his entire life. If there was a devil, as Candace was sure there was, then he was riding shotgun tonight with the Georgia State Police.

When it was all over, he was able to grip the steering wheel again. Candace said no more until he put the car in gear and started up.

"My goodness," she gasped through clenched teeth. "That was something, wasn't it?"

He nodded and laughed nervously and told her yes baby that certainly was something.

"I don't know about you, but I thought for sure that we were it." Candace shook her head and crossed her arms over her chest. He could only drive.

"I mean, my first thought was Julianne, that she'd told..."

It was honestly something he'd never considered, something that, in his fucking euphoria just a half an hour ago had almost completely forgotten about.

"...do you know?"

He was overcome with a suffocating dread.

"...and then my second thought..."

But she never got to finish her second thought 'cause he didn't slam the brakes on or anything like that he just said real quiet through clenched teeth what are you talking about.

Candace's jaw dropped and hung there, she was surprised that the same idea hadn't come to him and shocked that he could forget in the first place.

And while he waited on her answer, he sweated some more and he trembled some and he checked the rearview mirror for more cops and his eyes even squinted a little in anticipation of that fucking light. And then she said it plain as day, like it was obvious from the start and how could anybody not know this?

"Julianne was my best friend...well, man, I guess I've known her since the second grade, why, we–"

He went dumb with fear, and she, seeing what sort of state this news had thrown him into, went into a rage.

"I thought you knew that! Why else would I care if she seen me or not? I asked you... remember? I asked you and you said no, she didn't see me!"

So Julianne had seen her best friend

"...ex best friend..."

along with some strange man in the alleyway behind the house just before finding her dead husband upstairs. And Candace's daddy, well, he had the address of where his daughter was living and he'd seen the bastard sitting out there in the car waiting for her.

"I thought you knew! I told you! I DID!"

He could have killed her–Julianne–when he had the chance, and

dammit!

now she was probably sitting cozy in the police station, spilling her guts to some crisis counselor and fingering his bride-to-be. And those state police, they'd barely have time to finish their coffee before they were back out on the highway, looking for them. Only they'd find 'em quick now 'cause they'd seen him, they'd looked into the eyes of a fucking murderer and they just up and let him go with a warning about a broken taillight, hell, they didn't even write a ticket.

They would be plenty pissed the next time around.

"Maybe we should just keep goin', you know? Maybe we should go Texas, or New Orleans. I got family there... I think."

It was something to consider.

"We got enough money to make it to New Orleans?"

He shook his head and eased the car off the shoulder and back up onto the highway.

His speed picked up and he could not take his mind off of Julianne. Fuck the taillight; he found himself passing RVs and refrigerated semi-trucks as they barreled toward the Florida state line and headed for home to do some serious thinking about where to go from here. Get home, get Joe, marry Candace, and then what...? Maybe L.A.

First, they stopped at a rest area so he could wipe himself off and find that extra pair of pants in the back.

They had been silent for the twenty minutes it took to get to there, and even when they pulled into the parking lot, each said nothing, each scouting their own side of the lot for patrol cars and other suspicious-looking vehicles.

Satisfied that they were alone, he pulled into the last space on the right and parked so that the nose of the car pointed right for the onramp back to the highway. There were no other cars in the lot, but over on the far left of the asphalt clearing were five or six semi-trucks, all parked diagonally and placed neatly in a row with just a few feet of space between them.

He wished he were crashed in the back of one of them, babysitting a load of cattle on the way to slaughter or something easy like that.

He and Candace got out of the car, she wanted to let the dog loose so that he could sniff around in the damp grass and take a pee and as soon as she pushed the front seat up and out of the way, he took off and scampered into the thick bushes behind the restrooms where people sneak away and fuck on long trips.

The night got hotter the further south they drove. The cool breeze they had felt earlier stopped just as suddenly as the car did, and he could feel the damp stickiness under his arms and down his back returning. Though this stretch of road was sparsely populated, there was one house set off from the road about a hundred feet ahead. Through the living room came the dead blue light of the TV, and when no cars were passing by on the highway, the night echoed with the hysterical, exaggerated shrieks of canned laughter for some stupid program.

He stood alone between the men's and ladies' rooms and watched that house and pictured himself sitting in a recliner in the living room with the dog sleeping at his feet, nodding off just as the late show came on. He could hear a faceless crowd whooping with laughter and then the TV theme that the whole world screws to.

Lucky bastards.

The slamming of the trunk woke him out of the dream, and then there was Candace's silhouette walking barefoot across the greasy parking lot, picking her way over little pebbles and broken glass. She handed him the jeans and nodded toward the ladies' room.

"Men's is outta order. C'mon, come with me."

She pulled him away from the drone of the television and he went with her, even though all he really wanted to do was sit in the grass and listen to those programs in the night, hear the news and the late show and all those other things that regular folks do on a night such as this.

Inside the ladies' room, it stank of stale perfume and urine and he was surprised, like it should smell like antiseptic and have little pink rugs and matching toilet seat covers or something like that.

There were two sinks, one overflowing with water though the faucet was not turned on, and a row of four stalls along one wall. There was no toilet paper in any of them, and only two even had doors. If Candace were a man, he'd have just pissed in the sink, but instead he took the stall on the left, she, the one on the right.

He stood, feet pushed apart and shoulders drooped, reading the secrets of women that were scribbled across the tile in lipstick and Magic Marker.

I LOVE DONNA.

He arched one eyebrow and read some more.

SUSAN LOVES PAULIE 4EVER.

Mrs. Bobby Lee.

In pink lipstick,

MEN CAN FUCK THEMSELVES.

And then, in another shade of red,

IF THEY COULD, THEY'LL KILL EVERY ONE OF US.

He squeezed his eyes shut and waited but was finding it hard to concentrate. It was cramped and stuffy inside the damp bathroom stall, it smelled bad and there were all those damnations from females just passing through. The putty-colored metal partition was smeared on all four sides, and the lock on the door didn't work properly so it kept bumping him in the ass and trying to open.

He felt awkward and tried not to read the walls, the things written hastily but prophetically, like fucking scripture, and all cluttered up by peach lipgloss kisses and caked-up mascara and menstrual blood and Jesus, women are nasty creatures when they wanna be.

Collecting Candace

That small, dank bathroom stall held their secrets like some kind of shrine; he could have had his eyes put out so that he could see no more.

REPORT RAPE.

I LOVE BILLY T.

Those cops were probably out there now, circling the rest area and sweeping the night with that bright, white light.

I'M A PUSSY LICKER.

"Are you sorry you ever met me?"

He was silent, trying hard for just another second, when she asked him again.

"Are you? Sorry, I mean?"

He asked her, why, have you been bad? and with a weary, sarcastic laugh he pushed the door open with his heel and backed out, not bothering to zip up while he moved over to the sink to where his clean pants lay all folded up on the edge, in the only dry spot in the whole fucking place.

"I want to tell you something."

He'd been with her nearly three days now and in that short time they'd shared plenty, and now he thought, he was gonna get some of those things the others had taken, she was gonna tell him secrets about herself and he would not be a fool about it. He would not squander these things like the others had. Only, he wasn't sure he was ready to hear what Candace might be thinking about all of this.

He faced himself in the mirror, something that he had been careful not to do since that first night when they came back home after Bobby Lee's house. The stall where she sat was over his left shoulder in the reflection and his eyes moved over to the closed metal door and he listened to her sorrowful voice coming from inside. It echoed loudly in the wet, stale air. He leaned onto one hand on the edge of the wet sink and pushed one of his boots off.

"Do you know the worst thing I ever done?"

Do you want a pen?

Before he could ask, she changed the subject.

"What's the worst thing you ever done?"

He asked her to go first.

Her ankles, wrapped loosely in pink panties, were visible under the door—her bare feet too, her toes were all tanned and dirty peeking out under a rumpled heap of washed-out blue jeans. He watched her feet slide back and forth aimlessly while she talked, watched them picking up all kind of germs and things from the filth she was stepping in.

It was nasty all right but nasty was getting to be a subjective thing.

"I've been thinking about you."

He sighed and pushed the other boot off, then both his socks and then he stood in front of the mirror and let the mysterious puddles of liquid on the tile floor seep in between his toes. Candace was silent, and he stewed awkwardly as he tried to imagine the thoughts Candace might have about him. He just said uh-huh and tried not to seem overly interested but inside was twisting to hear the rest.

He shimmied out of his stiff, wet jeans, pushing them down over his hips. The soaked denim scraped his flesh as it slid over his thighs, and not till they fell off his body completely, in a musty, stinky heap around his ankles did he realize how constricting they really were. It felt good to be without them. He stepped out of them and kicked them aside and again took stock of his reflection, now clad only in a pair of Jockey shorts and a damp, white T-shirt.

"The things you said, about you and me being together, they were beautiful. And they got me to thinking about what it would really be like...about what it's really gonna be like."

His gaze darted to the metal door where Candace was hiding and he blushed like a seventh-grader.

"I think it's gonna be nice." Even under wraps in the bathroom stall, her voice was soft and self-conscious.

He thought of her, thinking of him, and he flexed his muscles once and smiled to himself.

"The way you've made me feel, inside, I mean..."

He winked at himself with cocky bravado but was secretly eating this up and wanted to hear more. He struck another pose, this time flexing his chest muscles, and when he saw the slight rippling beneath the thin cotton of his T-shirt, he shucked it as well and stood, now nearly nude, in front of the scratched-up mirror above the sink.

He was a warrior.

A *fucking fighter.*

Reveling in the hunt, the chase, the tribal kill that would appease the gods but probably not Jesus.

She was silent, but he didn't say anything yet, he knew he wasn't supposed to. Instead, he just watched his own reflection and felt a little silly but hell, it was just a game and besides, he looked strong like this, and he liked that. He felt strong too. He grinned lewdly and turned slightly so that he could see the muscles in his back as well and the sight of it pleased him.

"Nobody's ever made me feel like that before,"

He didn't think of her three ex-husbands. He just smiled like a fat cat and slapped his flat belly with his open palm, just like you do after a big meal and he felt that same satisfaction. He felt like The Man Around Here.

Candace's pink panties disappeared from sight as they climbed her shins; a second later her legs straightened, but she did not come out. Instead, she sat down again and continued.

"I think that the worst thing I ever did was let you kill Danny Ray and Bobby Lee."

This did not bode well for him. The grin was still there, only it looked stupid now. He forced it to stay put there on his face and he wasn't about to go pitching a fit or getting all excited, but he wished the subject would go back to sex, or at least back to those warm feelings she was getting at. He wished she would tell him a joke; her jokes were so dumb but you had to love the way she told them. Brother, he thought, we could use a good joke right now.

He laid his palms across his chest and felt the healing scratches there; most had been left by Danny Ray though a couple were hers as well. His fingertips moved over his torn-up skin and in certain places it still stung. There was a thin line of dried-up blood just across his ribs, on the left side, but most all of the other stains had been washed away by his sweat. He felt the wounds and guessed where the scars would stay and where they would eventually fade over time.

So this is what it's come to, hiding out in the girls' bathroom.

"Actually," she corrected herself. "The worse thing I ever done was be glad that you killed Danny Ray and Bobby Lee."

It was a relief to hear that, and he guessed it was probably a relief for her to say it.

"I bet you think that's terrible, that I could wish something like that, wish for someone to be dead."

It was terrible, that's what he was thinking, but it's not what he said 'cause he was not without sin himself.

"It's awful, I know it. You don't have to tell me. You know what? Sometimes... I have a hard time being happy for people, 'specially when things are going their way." She paused. "I almost didn't come back, to the motel, I mean."

He wanted to tell her that she needn't have worried, that not much was going his way that night or any other recent night but instead, he bent over the sink, the one that was not overflowing with dirty water, and turned the cold water on but the best it could do was tepid, so he splashed some of that over his face and then over his naked chest too, enjoying the feel of it trickling over his sores and down his belly. Practically the only wet he felt since this whole thing began was from sweat but this felt good. His hand came up and caressed his cheek; it was thickly coated with black stubble and he thought that he'd love to have a shave right now.

"Anyway, that's it. That's the worst thing I ever done." She stood behind the metal door and he could almost see her, fondling the handle and waiting for him to share his piece.

"What about you?"

He balled the white T-shirt up in his broad, calloused hands and held it under the tap and soaked it good and then wrung it out and slapped it over his bare legs.

He told her he could just as easily have killed her as have fucked her. And that, he told her, was the worst thing he'd ever done. God's honest truth. And then he put his pants on and his socks and his boots and she laughed suddenly from inside the bathroom stall.

"Wasn't that the stupidest joke you ever heard? The dead monkey?"

He smiled fondly at the memory and agreed with her yes, it was one of the worst jokes he ever did hear.

"'Cause it was dead..." Her voice trailed off and she chuckled again and even he did this time, remembering how damn silly she looked that night, carrying on about the dead thing falling out a tree and hard as he tried he couldn't remember the one about the dog with no legs. Neither could she but she was sure it wasn't as funny.

She came out just as he was trying to slide that soaking wet shirt down his torso.

They stood toe-to-toe in the girls' room, like in the hallway that night and she wasn't afraid to come real close, though she should've been, especially after being told such a thing as he told her. She should have been scared then too but come to think of it there weren't very many things that seemed to fright-

Collecting Candace

en Candace. Leastways, not in the real world. She only smiled and rested her hands on his chest, feeling the cool material under her touch. It was warm where her hands were, but he didn't mind. It wasn't the same kind of hot that was waiting for them out there, out at the other end of that highway.

Wordlessly, she bent her head and pressed her cheek into the drenched cotton, sponging up the moisture with her flesh and hoping it would lower her body temperature and it felt good for both of them.

"I guess, if you look at the big picture, you know, if you look at your life as a whole, then neither one of them things is really so bad, even for being the worst...do you think?"

He smiled down at the top of her head and he thought no this girl ain't stupid and probably no man who's ever bedded her knew that.

"Ready to go home?" she asked, without looking up. He felt a gentle vibration in his chest when she spoke and he liked it so much that he didn't answer her the first time; he knew she would ask again, which she did.

This time he said yes, he was ready and she took his hand and led him outside and then whistled for the dog. The highway still lay there in the distance but it was not so far away this time. Neither was Gainesville, just a few more hours.

In just a few minutes, they were back out on the road and headed for home, feeling a little nervous, a little relieved, anxious about what tomorrow would bring, and for the first time since their journey began, not so hot.

chapter eight

Because of what was coming for them in the next twelve hours, the little peace they could share on the last leg to Gainesville would be something that would stand out forever when recalling these days, though this was not something they were aware of at the time. For it was soon after that things in general would begin to go badly. They would continue doing so until it was damn difficult, if not impossible, to set things right again.

Even while the state of Florida was pronouncing them man and wife, he was dressing out Just Plain Joe in the back of his mind and keeping one watchful eye on the door where the police were most likely to crash through, though they did not. While he kissed the bride he could think only of those cold steel bracelets clamping down around his wrists and pinching his flesh, and he missed out entirely on the sensation of kissing his wife for the very first time.

It was some trip.

Prob'ly should've done Disneyworld.

They were both getting tired and there was no doubt they were happy to be out of Georgia, state police and all things considered. Just when they were almost home and this close crawling into bed, things took a turn for the worse, as they were apt to do lately, and spiraled right straight to hell.

Collecting Candace

He knew the moment he said it

What all have you got in there, the baby fucking Jesus?

that he shouldn't have; she needn't have slapped him so hard but she did. Religion just seemed to rub Candace the wrong way.

It was just a joke, but there was no use trying to tell her that now and even if he had she would not have gotten it anyway. He never even would have thought to say it, only she looked so cute rummaging through her bag for what—he didn't even remember—and spilling out all sorts of girl crap onto the seat between them. Dusty breath mints, picture postcards, lipstick and yarn (he'd never seen her knit anything) and a sewing kit too and when he saw the can opener that's when he said it

the baby fucking Jesus?

and that's when she slapped him.

What he did next, he also knew was a mistake, but the past three days had finally taken their toll and despite their undying devotion there was almost nothing he could do to arrest the tension that was coming between them.

He ripped that Blessed Virgin Mary off the dash of the Maverick and tossed it right out the window.

She didn't scream or say anything; she opened her mouth like she was gonna but then clamped her hand down over it and watched the tiny Mother of God bounce along in the red glow of the one good taillight. Once She was out of sight, Candace turned for him and slapped him once, hard. Then she slid back toward her side of the car and stuffed everything back into her bag and put on a look. He knew that both Bobby Lee and Danny Ray had probably seen that look often and if that weren't enough, he realized with a horror that from now on, in Candace's mind, what he'd just done would always be remembered as The Blessed Virgin Mary Incident No. 2.

He rolled his eyes in surrender and groaned.

Lord, take me now.

His brain geared up for another mind fuck

nothin' like gettin' some

but the rest of him just couldn't find the strength. One look into her eyes and he could see nothing but bad things ahead. There had been more than a couple of times he'd wished he'd stayed in bed and slept her off, and at that minute he was thinking that's just what I shoulda done, but he was in deep now and if there was one thing he learned from Bobby Lee it was that it really didn't matter what you should have done.

He sighed and told her come on baby don't be mad but she wouldn't budge. Between stealing glimpses at the road ahead he watched her profile and felt a whole new set of bad feelings overtake him. Betrayal stung him deep. It wasn't her losing her temper so much or even the slap that hurt, it was that she was sitting over there thinking not about how to make it up to him, but more likely about when she could get back this way to find that fucking statuette.

He wanted to say enough is enough and where was Jesus when those state troopers were breathing down our necks he sure as hell was not in the front seat of this car. Hell, it would have just made her that much madder, and she would've held on that

Collecting Candace

much tighter. And Mary. What did that goddamned little statue do other than give her nightmares and remind her of the mother who left her behind? And even if they could help, if they could grab a flight to Florida, would they want to? Well, hell, no 'cause no one was there to stop him that night in the motel and if it was like Candace said it was, then it wouldn't matter none if she prayed and he did not.

He was the one with blood under his fingernails and he was the one who they were gonna hang and he was the one who was getting so he couldn't sleep no more and now, when he needed her loving him more than ever she goes and slaps him and makes him feel like shit for doing something that should have been long forgotten a quarter of a mile down the road.

Jesus Saves.

Well, so does fucking Datsun as the saying used to go but try telling that to Candace.

He thought he might just get mad right back at her and even thought about stopping the car and shoving her ass right out onto the road but he couldn't. He just told her again please baby don't be mad over nothing at all but her lips were all pinched together and she was looking like there was cereal milk somewhere in that car.

It wasn't that it was getting hard to love Candace anymore, and for some reason, wantin' to just got easier and easier. But this girl was a piece of work like he'd never seen and all that came along with her was a real bitch to get a grip on.

He figured it was supply and demand that, where she come from, put such a high price on forgiveness.

She stared straight ahead and pouted and part of him just said well fuck her but it was not the part that would say so.

Turning around and going back for the Mary was no good; the night was nearly pitch black and there was no way they'd find the thing and goddamn if he was gonna get on his knees on the side of the road for Her.

When he slowed the car at one point to let some road creature cross the highway, Candace tried to jump out the passenger side and run away. She got the door open and was not quite hanging halfway out but this time he would not let her go. He dug his fingers into her wrist and held on tight and hollered out into the still Florida night that he would not be left alone with himself again and that he loved her too much to let things fall to pieces when they were so close to having it all.

He yanked her back inside and then leaned across her lap to slam the door shut and lock it and he told her goddamnit don't you ever pull no stunt like that again you coulda been killed.

She cried some, and he felt like shit again but hell, hadn't they been through a time together? He'd cried too back there on the highway. At Bobby Lee's as well. Didn't mean a thing. Coulda been low blood sugar or some such malaise. Fuck. Might as well have been the heat, which was back hotter than ever. Hotter than hell, it surely was. He knew, 'cause he'd just come from there and it was nothing compared to the hot he was feeling in that car.

He said once more that he was real sorry for

Collecting Candace

throwing Her out onto that stretch of road. And he meant it too and for a minute he wondered if he could go to hell for that.

They were just about to his house where he could have put the whole thing to bed when Candace said well prove it that you're sorry and make a right turn right here, which he did, not realizing at the moment that he was driving the two of them right straight down the aisle.

If it were not for the painted plywood Cupid that was nailed to a beam just above the porch, he would have never guessed that the place she'd brought him to was a wedding chapel. It was a house like any other, and there was no organ music pumping through the windows; nor did the smell of orange blossom waft through the air on a gentle breeze. There was nothing, save for that smirking bastard with the bow and arrow, that would indicate what went on inside.

The More the Marryer Wedding Chapel.

He'd heard of this place before, from friends who'd stood witness for others and from locals who liked to poke fun about the pot-smoking justice of the peace who ran it. It was best described as a sort of connubial five-and-dime, on account of the types who were usually united there. Youngsters who knew no better, couples already twice divorced from one another but willing to give it another go, and on Saturday nights, men who were delirious with gin and love, in that order.

Wedding chapels are not like tattoo parlors, which are morally bound to refuse service to those under the influence; Rev. Bob had a sense of humor, that much could be said, and as long as the proper license had been obtained, the More the Marryer would join anyone, anytime, and if you were too drunk to know what you were doing then his reply was always Take it up with her, not me.

Candace leapt first. She bolted right out of the passenger side door and stomped up the stairs two at a time, and then rapped loudly on the door while he sat silently in the car, peering out the snotted-up windshield and sweating.

He'd never been married, never even been to a real wedding and subsequently knew nothing about what it, the actual marrying part, would be like. Having laid eyes upon this plain house set back in the woods, not to mention that naked winged thing that stood above them, he remembered pictures of wedding chapels in Vegas and wished it were more like one of those, not with a preacher who dressed like Elvis or anything like that, just a little bit more dressed-up and kind of fancy-looking.

It was, after all, till death they do part.

It was, of course, not the actual setting of their wedding that bothered him so much as the event itself. And how she could go in just five minutes from slapping him to marrying him was just another one of those girl mysteries, along with prerogative, a word he'd come to know intimately.

Hard as he tried to get excited over being married, he could not take his thoughts off of Joe and of wondering where he was at this moment and did he have any idea what would be coming his way. Was it on the news already and would he be in hiding? Would the cops be waiting for him at Joe's place or

Collecting Candace

was he just flattering himself with such thoughts? He wished they'd gotten that last visit out of the way before coming here, for nothing would set right, not the vows or the promises or anything, until Candace's slate was clean.

Stuck between proving his love for her and proving something else entirely to himself, he waffled in the car, unable to get out, unwilling to drive away, until Candace noticed him hanging back and waved excitedly for him to join her, which he did, reluctantly.

The heat was even worse close to the house. Next to the smell of chicken coming from inside, it was the first thing he noticed when he took his place alongside Candace. He was sweating something awful but she seemed to not even notice the heat. He pulled the crewneck of his T-shirt away from his skin but it stuck there like paste and he knew, now that they were back in Florida, it would just get hotter and hotter.

The night all around had been quiet, and he'd enjoyed what break they'd had, but here, the peace of the woods was broken by talk radio coming from inside the house. That, and the mindless conversation of caged parakeets. Mixed together, it was a sound that made him want to cut off his own ears and bury them in the dirt. He hoped they'd have some records to play when the time for marrying finally came, but not the Carpenters, Lord that was real girl crap.

The front door was open, but the screen door was not, and they could peer inside at the yellow light that came from some far corner of the living room. From what he could see, it looked like anyone else's house, books stacked here and there, some old shoes thrown up against the wall by the front door and some unopened bills on a small oak table in the front entryway. No pews or wreaths of flowers. No altar either, from what he could make out. The radio, still playing, was not visible either, on account of the layout of the house. He could hear it though, and he could see somebody's bare feet propped up on a table and bobbing aimlessly to a tune that wasn't there.

Candace looked at him and shrugged and this time he knocked, but still those feet did not move, except in the rhythmic way they had before.

The heavy, funky aroma of marijuana settled over the front porch like a fog and that explained a lot.

He remembered that his sister had gotten married on a cruise ship with five hundred witnesses. The ceremony was performed by the captain and she said they all threw little flower blossoms into the sea afterward and then had complimentary champagne. He knocked once more.

He was thinking about Joe and feeling that none of this was right. He tried to think of a gentle way to say these feelings he was having but there was none so he just plain said maybe we should come back another time.

She was silent for a good long time and it gave them both time to think on what to do next. Candace, she was more likely thinking how hard she was going to hit him and where but he was reeling with stupid regret at having tainted this moment for her. He should have been down on his knees and instead

Collecting Candace

he was on his belly.

Luckily, Rev. Bob opened the door just in time and decided for both of them just the way that things would be.

Rev. Bob of course knew Candace, and the two of them made a big commotion over seeing one another again.

He hung back in the shadows of the front porch and did not speak until spoken to, and even then, only to cough up a nervous hello and a half-hearted how are you?

The preacher's wife was there too, she came trotting out of the kitchen, her hands slick with raw chicken and the whole front of her body dusted with flour. She too hugged Candace and then shook his hand and they all stepped into the light of the living room to sign all the paperwork and make sure everything was on the up and up with the state of Florida.

He still hadn't said anything about Joe specifically and how things were supposed to have worked out, even when Candace disappeared into the other room with the preacher and the preacher's wife went upstairs to find something nice for her to wear, he was left alone with his thoughts and still did not have the voice to stop this.

It would have been one thing to turn the car around when he had the chance, it would have even been all right—though cutting it close—to say something when they were standing out there on the front porch, but bringing it up now would amount to nothing less that jilting her at the altar, which was a sin so unthinkable he had to purposely squeeze it right out of his mind.

He wandered around the living room aimlessly, looking at the record album collection and a stack of anarchist books that lay on the coffee table and he finally took a seat in the entry hall, just off the second bedroom, where Candace and Rev. Bob were laughing and reminiscing like old acquaintances do.

Next to the kitchen, the entry hall was probably the hottest room in the house; it was small too, maybe five foot square, but the living room stank of marijuana and the radio was too loud in there and he didn't want to sit in the kitchen, so he chose the seat on the hall tree. It was an oak platform that was barely wide enough for him to fit.

He perched himself on the edge and plugged one ear so's not to hear the moaning of some girl whose husband was a drunkard.

The sleepy voice of a radio psychologist crooned over the airwaves. "...I think I can save this marriage, I think I can help you but you're gonna have to help yourself first..."

to a shotgun maybe

and Candace chatted gleefully in the next room as she recollected something funny that had happened years before he met her. He fidgeted in his seat. He sat erect, and his spine rubbed annoyingly against the hardwood backing of the hall tree, but it was so fucking hot and so goddamned stuffy, he didn't have the strength to get up and walk around again. A fly buzzed around his head and he slapped it against his cheek and watched it fall to the nubby carpet.

Hanging on the wall, directly across from him

Collecting Candace

and in plain sight, was a small mirror that framed
his face just perfectly from where he sat. It upset him
that his hair was so mussed up and he wondered why
nobody had given him a comb when they'd seen it.

"...he's got to ask for help, he's got to want it...
more'n you, more'n anything..."

Sweat dripped down his back and he scooted out
to the edge of the seat and pinched a section of T-
shirt and waved it some, so that some air could get
back there and dry him off.

A bird screamed from the squalor of its cage
somewhere off in the house.

"...and he wore that awful blue suit! Oh, my
God, I'd almost forgotten about that!" Candace
howled again from the other room and as much as he
loved the sound of her laughter, it stuck in his craw
tonight and it pissed him off to hear the preacher's
stupid, stoned guffaws after every damn thing she
said, funny or not.

The chicken was burning. He could smell it. He
looked up the stairs for the preacher's wife but she
was nowhere in sight, so he listened to the Crisco
popping and snapping in the fry pan.

He smoothed his damp bangs back with the
palm of his hand, bounced his knee and thought that
he sure did look a sight for a man who was about to
get married. He cocked his head and arched one eyebrow and stared at his reflection and tried to imagine himself as half of anything, but he guessed that
it would take some getting used to. His eyes drooped
and his lips were red, like they were chapped, and
then suddenly the preacher's wife appeared out of
nowhere, carrying a white gauze dress. She passed

through the foyer and interrupted his thoughts, accidentally bumping his knees trying to get by, on account of her being so large. He swung them to the right and jerked his gaze away from the mirror but it was too late. She smiled fondly like she'd caught him being nervous and he said excuse me ma'am and turned away.

"Would you like a cup of coffee?" Her puffy, sweaty face peered down at his with kindness and squinty eyes but all he could think was no goddamit it's a hundred and fucking eighty degrees in here shove the coffee up your ass. Instead, he politely said no thank you and when she asked him if he'd like a beer, he said yes.

She returned minutes later with a can of beer and nodded toward the room where Candace and Rev. Bob were.

"It won't be long now," she said and then she left again, wiping her hands on her belly as she disappeared into the kitchen.

He stiffened when he thought of Candace in there dressing and he thought that fucking room had better have another door in it and just then, as if reading his jealous thoughts, the preacher came out, closed the door behind and offered him a cigarette, which he took and lighted himself with a book of matches that he fished out of his back pocket, tucked between the folds of the construction paper.

"Candace sure is something," Rev. Bob chuckled as he shook his head. "Known her, oh, a long, long time. We go way back."

He avoided looking at the preacher, 'cause doing so caused him to tighten the muscles in his face and he waited for the bastard to say something like Gotta love her, but he did not.

He took a drag of the cigarette and then stood and excused himself to finish his smoke outside and the preacher called after him don't be too nervous she knows what to do and then he laughed at his own joke.

This pissed him off even more but he let it go, just happy to be out of the house where the parakeets were sounding murderous by now and the radio psychologist was surely full of shit.

"...now, listen to me, listen to me, you make a covenant to one another, the two of you, are you listening? You have to make a promise, to yourselves, to..."

The screen door squeaked and then slammed shut and it scared the birds like it was one of their own in peril, setting them off on another tirade. The dog was off stalking bugs in the dry grass.

It was somewhat cooler outside, though not by much, but he was glad to not feel so suffocated. He kicked up some dust with his boots as he moved away from the porch, listening to the sounds inside quiet down some, and he came to stop just underneath the plywood Cupid, holding the half-smoked cigarette in one hand and the warm beer that the preacher's wife gave him in the other.

He thought of Candace in there having a time, well, hell, it was her wedding night and she should have fun, but he couldn't help but feel so jealous. Not at the way that others loved her, but at the way she so easily loved them all back.

She wasn't thinking about how fucking hot it

was and she wasn't wondering where Joe was right now. It probably didn't even enter her mind, not since Georgia anyway, that the police might be looking for them. All she knew was that she was gonna be someone's bride.

He was wanting to piece it all together in his mind just once more, wanting to find the logic in what he was planning on doing later that night, but it was too late to think about. Like when gators gotta cross a crowded highway. They don't stop to think about it 'cause if when they do... splat. They just go on instinct. Cars or none. They just go.

The beer was warm but he drank it just the same. He took the last drag of his Pall Mall and stared up at the winged boy above him. That thing was a sorry-looking advertisement if he'd ever seen one, and if this were the sight that was gonna lure people toward the act of matrimony, then surely half the state of Florida would still be single. The tip of the arrow was pointed straight at his nose and that Cupid, if he'd a mind to, could have sent it right through his brain.

Sleeping on the tracks

He just had to laugh it was so ironic.

Candace giggled from inside the house and he fought to keep the faith she'd promised him. Seeing her happy, hearing her laugh inside there, while he stood out beneath the sky, alone, he couldn't help but think about all the people she'd touched and what they must be carrying around inside of them, things that she gave them for keeps. He couldn't help but wonder will it make a difference in the long run if he can't touch that stuff.

Collecting Candace

It was incredible to him that she came out of the house when she did, because he was just wishing she would, right at that moment. It was a sign. The sight of her bounding down the front stairs in that sheer white dress, looking like some kind of angel, was enough to lift his heart right out of the pit it had sunk into.

He tossed the beer can onto the ground and opened his arms wide for her and she slid right in, wrapping her arms around his waist and nuzzling his cheek with her soft, pink lips.

The night was wide open and they could have gone anywhere, could have done anything. All she had to do was pull the car keys from his pocket and say let's go. But instead, she led him back up the stairs toward where the piano music was coming from

I love you truly

and he went, with a heavier heart than he'd had just a moment ago but still grateful that she had chosen him.

It was a nice ceremony and Rev. and Mrs. Bob even threw rice afterward. Some of it got into his ears and his eyes but it was the thought that counted.

Afterward, Rev. Bob pulled him aside and offered him a joint and said there's a lot of talk and that whatever their plan is they better get on with it and get out of Florida. And don't go back to Georgia.

This was not news to him. He knew it was coming and he told the Rev. so and he also told him that they were leaving that night, maybe to L.A. as soon as he was able to get some of his stuff from home, but Rev. Bob told him better not try it. The cops are probably there now.

Just as they were getting into the car, Rev. Bob's wife leaned her head into the driver's side window of the Maverick and gave him a kiss on the cheek and said God Bless. And then she asked for his autograph, which he gave to her, inside of her white Bible, the only thing handy to write on.

They headed out of there for no place in particular, but stopped a few hundred yards from the house when Candace produced a bottle of wine that Preacher Bob had given her and with which she wanted to toast her new marriage. Even he could not refuse.

They pulled off the dirt road and under the shade of some low-hanging trees. Off in the distance they could hear dogs barking at sounds in the night. The dog whined longingly to join them but soon settled down in the back seat and found his bed again.

Husband and wife. Mr. and Mrs. They smiled at each another and blushed and it felt strange to suddenly belong to this person, with all that went with it, but it felt nice. They had no wine glasses, so they took turns taking swigs from the bottle and while one drank, the other would set forth the rules of the marriage as he or she saw them, and then vice versa.

Love, honor, and cherish me is how it began, but because of the late hour, and the wine, it soon turned into a game that was the most fun they'd had in days. Don't pick your nose at the dinner table and don't pee in the shower.

Collecting Candace

They laughed and dribbled chablis down their chins and they made an awful racket out there in the woods at nearly three a.m., but it was all right and it didn't matter any what they did anymore, 'cause they were married now.

Married.

He didn't even mind the heat so much, though it was still there and for sure he still felt it. But the soothing sound of crickets in the night and the gentle buzz in his head from the wine and from Candace made that night one of the best in his whole life. A couple of times he heard noises in the woods around them, snaps and pops like someone walking on sticks and it occurred to him that that could be them now, that they could be surrounding the car, just like in that movie, *Bonnie and Clyde*.

He smiled at the comparison and turned to tell Candace how funny it was, but she was curled up against the passenger side door and falling asleep. Too much excitement. He stroked her bare calf with his palm and nudged her gently, whispering to her you got anymore of those dumb jokes and without even opening her eyes she said yes.

"Oh, I got a good one! What did the dumb blond say when her doctor told her she's pregnant?"

He smiled in anticipation of the punch line and shook his head and said what.

"Is it mine?" she giggled.

This he found even funnier than the dead monkey and he laughed for a full minute. Candace snickered too and he asked for another.

"Why did the dumb blond get fired outta the M&M factory?"

He squeezed Candace's bare, dirty foot and said tell me.

"For throwing out all the ones with W's."

She was on a roll and she was enjoying the attention, which he was glad to give her. He leaned his head back on the head rest and even enjoyed the smell of the hot, wet Florida night. He was having the best time in the world and wanted it to go on forever. His attention was fully on Candace, who was remembering a few more pretty good jokes and though she messed up a coupla punch lines, he laughed all the same.

He took another long drink of wine and offered it to her but she shook her head no and said I'm wasted.

This was better than the drive down from Georgia. It was hot tonight, hotter than it was then, but there was more to be thankful for tonight and the memories that were still fresh in their minds were nicer too.

He patted his packet of cigarettes that was rolled up in his sleeve and remembered the joint that Rev. Bob had given him just after he'd been paid the fifteen dollars.

He took it out and lit it and took a long, slow drag, holding the potent smoke in for as long as he could. It stank up the car some but Christ it tasted good. After getting married, after the wine, after a day as long as they'd had, it was perfect. It was ecstasy. He offered it to Candace and she roused herself up just enough to take a hit. And then she remembered another joke.

"Why did the dumb blond write TGIF on her shoes?"

Collecting Candace

He started to giggle uncontrollably, whether it was the wine or the weed or what, he didn't know, but he laughed and told her hurry up tell me.

"Toes Go in First."

He howled with laughter into the dark, quiet night and Candace, pleased that she could be so funny, burst into giggles too. They laughed for ten minutes at this last joke; when he would start to slow down and catch his breath, she would start up again, and vice versa. Finally, when their stomachs ached and their eyes were watering and they couldn't laugh no more, he lifted the joint to his lips and said damn my hands smell like raw chicken and they started to howling all over again.

Even the dog enjoyed the camaraderie. He stuck his wet nose between the two front seats and panted gleefully and Candace said look, he's smiling. The dog, in fact, did seem to be smiling. He had every right to.

They took another hit off the weed and then pinched the end till it was no longer burning and then stuck what was left of it into the ashtray for safekeeping. Candace had grown sleepy and was curled up against the passenger side door and when he asked her for another one she said I got plenty where those came from I'll tell you tomorrow now get some sleep.

Who knew how much time they had passed sitting and drinking that wine and getting high and how much more he had spent just watching her sleep. Logic, and Rev. Bob, had told him he'd better hightail it outta of the great state of Florida as soon as possible, but he seemed cemented to this one spot of the woods, and to this one place in time. This was how he wanted to spend every night for the rest of his life, laughing with Candace and telling jokes and feeling all their problems just go away in a puff of smoke and the only thing that was missing now was making love to her and that would be easy.

He watched her body in the moonlight, the way it was all illuminated up and down her thigh and her calf, like it was that first night when the TV lighted her in the house. His hand moved up to the spot behind her knee and he cupped her there and felt how warm it was and it was wonderful that she was his wife. He touched her thigh too and felt a tingling through his body at the thought of continuing. She fell asleep instantly and stayed that way, sleeping soundly. Her breathing was deep and even and steady and mixed with the sounds of the night, it was everything that peace should sound like. Peace of mind.

The Missus. How easy it would be to love her now. And how delicious. Except for one thing. Except for Joe. As much as he wanted her, and at that moment he wanted her like nothing that ever came before, he wanted her with a passion that erased everything he felt that night in the motel room. But even he knew that if he could take her now, then he could have loved her the first night and that would mean that what he'd done was in vain and for nothing at all. Just another senseless crime, like the kind you hear about on the TV news. If his logic was flawed from the start, then so it must be, but it was a plan they had vowed to follow from the beginning, and they had come too far to just abandon this path in favor of another easier, more convenient way.

In short, he had dug himself a hole which only he could dig himself out of, with the help, of course, of Bobby Lee, Danny Ray, and finally Just Plain Joe.

He sat still and sweated, watching her and weighing these thoughts in his mind and wanting so bad to travel the curves of that body. He could smell her, cigarettes and wine and perfume and dope and in the confines of that car, he could not escape his desire.

Will her friends turn him in and is this just like last time he was almost taken in, when all he could think about was that he wished he'd been inside of her just once.

It was a close call. They were already married and what came before, he'd handled as well. He'd done it like he said he would and in the process had left his own mark on her, created his own past so that he didn't just know things about her anymore, he knew her. He knew the look and he knew the voice that she used when she wanted him, or wanted anything. He knew things about her body, not how it looked or even felt but how it moved when it was happy or sad or scared and he wanted to make love to that body. To touch it, places like the outside of her hip and the soft flesh in the crook of her arm. It was the difference between sex and making love 'cause they weren't just doing things to one another, things they'd pleased others with. And she'd touch him, she'd put her hands on him and touch his heart, his soul, use her fingers to remember things they'd said to one another and use her lips to make him recall them too.

He knew all of this about her. And so then he knew that he must go now.

He woke her rudely and said come on we've got to get a move on we've got to finish this now.

She was groggy from lack of sleep and from the wine and so her resistance was practically nothing at all. She led them out of there, down some more back roads and behind the old schoolhouse and just when he was wondering where the hell she was leading him to, she told him to stop.

He wondered if she was drunk or what, for there were no houses were Candace stopped him. Here it was, almost four in the morning, and they appeared to be no closer to Joe than when they were back at Rev. Bob's, getting married, or even back at Bobby Lee's or Danny Ray's, for that matter. He was growing impatient and nervous and had hoped to be out of Gainesville by the time the sun came up, but, like he noticed before, there were no houses.

Only tombstones.

chapter nine

He scanned the stone markers that dotted the dead landscape that lay before him, and when Candace pointed toward the back, where it was dark

"There, over there."

his heart lost all hope that Just Plain Joe was tending graves or digging holes or some such chore.

He felt a drop of rain on the back of his neck and he absent-mindedly wiped it away, not even aware of the cool wet spot that it left behind. He reached into the back seat for a tire iron and Candace said you don't need that to talk to Joe but he wasn't altogether sure that's why he pulled it out in the first place.

She felt the next drop and looked toward the sky.

"Well, thank heaven, it's about time."

He slammed the door shut, and his palm skidded on the messy window. The dog got out just in time and went galloping off into a thicket where it would find things to eat.

He felt more drops on the top of his head and on the end of his nose, but it was of no comfort at all.

It was not a hard rain, it was not even a drizzle. It was just enough that when the fat drops hit the dirt all around their feet, it sent up tiny clouds of dust like bombardiers on target.

He ignored the faint cooling sensation as he pushed past the Maverick's front fender and stood before the closed gates of the cemetery. There were no words to give the impression he got when laying eyes for the first time on Joe's address. Though he tried not to jump to conclusions–Candace had, after all, not actually said Joe is dead and he is buried here–his hopeful wondering grew meek while watching the rows of graves fan out over the horizon.

To call it despair would have made him laugh. To say it was a void would have given that feeling a name and that would have been a grave injustice because once named, that's forever what it would be. And, as his mute, dumb expression clearly told, there was no word or gesture to fit his state of being at that moment.

Candace reached down and picked some wildflowers and motioned for him to follow.

"Come on, this is it. This is what you wanted to see..."

He did want to see. He needed to. He needed to see the words on a tombstone, to see the name and have her point at it and lounge on the soft mound of earth and caress it lovingly and then say this is Joe this is my husband. Until he could see it with his own eyes, he couldn't believe it. And his quest would never end.

The rain tried to come and cool the earth but relief was so infrequent; tonight would be no different. It fell sporadically onto his head and shoulders and onto the toes of his boots, where the drops left smears of clean where before there had only been layers of dust and maybe some dried blood. It fell onto the trees all around them and he could hear the soft whispering of leaves, slick with rainwater, brushing against one another.

He had, from the beginning, prayed for rain and now it had come and he wondered if his one answered prayer had been wasted. He hoped that Candace had not made the same appeal on his behalf. He hoped that she hadn't squandered her prayers and that maybe there would be an end to this after all. But she walked through the gates confidently and with purpose and he knew, in the pit of his heart, that she was leading him to her first husband's grave.

The grass was tall except for the few places where next of kin kept it mowed and neatly-trimmed. Crabgrass mostly, and dandelions. Maybe millions of dandelions. They sprang from the soil and reached up, like long fingers, grasping for his ankles as he walked past. Even through the thick blue denim, he could feel the soft wisps of wild weeds and those dense flowers as he pushed on and broke through their bright yellow barrier.

Though they were alone, he felt eyes turn toward them as they made their way straight toward the back of the graveyard. Candace went first, he followed right behind, leaving a path of flattened grass and dead flowers and the large iron gate swinging silently in the night.

They would occasionally pass under a low-hanging tree and it would give him a fright to be touched by a drooping twig. He waved away unseen bugs and other things that might come near as, more than once, something tickled his ear and sent him skipping closer up behind Candace.

The rain stopped for a beat and then started up again.

Starting at the base of his spine and slowly traveling upward through his entire body, he felt the most intense heat, like sulphur beneath his skin, and then he got the strangest sensation from the rain. When the drops came down and smacked against his exposed skin, they seemed to crackle and sizzle like that oil did when Rev. Bob's wife left her chicken unattended. He could smell his charred flesh in the musty rain like he smelled that burning dinner from the hallway, and with each drop that fell upon him, he looked and felt more and more like blackened Cajun chicken meat.

Candace's cool, slender fingers touched his forearm and he recoiled, of course not wanting to sear her flesh as well, but she did not feel it like he did.

"Come on, I'm tired..."

Dreams are so real sometimes, it's hard to know where one starts and another stops. Gray bars, a cell. It was no different. Imprisoned by what?

chains of love you stupid fuck

He dumbly let her take his hand and lead him on. It was hard to see, for the clouds that brought the rain had obscured the moonlight and they had to be careful to stay on the thinned out paths between the graves, following them like a hiking trail in the state park. Occasionally they would stray and trudge over a soft mound of grass and they might as well have been walking on hot coals, the way it affected him so.

The full impact of where they were going and

what they were about to see had not hit him, it had not even begun to make its presence known in his senses, like when the light hit him that first time, there was only a dull expectation of something big coming his way. His gaze bounced from grave marker to grave marker, occasionally he'd pick up a stray name or date

beloved Mother, in the company of angels

but he tried not to look.

The tire iron dangled loosely in his right hand, and when Candace made a sharp turn to avoid hitting a giant cement St. Augustine, he was swung around too far, sending the tip of his weapon into the corner of a modest headstone and accidentally chipping off a piece.

He could not help but think that if the police were to corner him here they would piss off a lot of next-of-kin.

Near his feet, just off to the left, was a large rectangle of pressed, wet dirt where a grave marker, which had most likely been repossessed from some poor soul, used to be.

They walked for what seemed like hours, but in reality, it was only his suspended state of mind that made their journey feel endless.

They picked their way through a maze of stillborn babies and crippled grandfathers, through cancerous remains and victims of their own self-treachery, so by the time that he and Candace had reached row eighteen, where she promised they would find Joe, he was overcome by a queer combination of repulsion and empowerment.

There was a measure of shame, especially when

Collecting Candace

he thought of Danny Ray and Bobby Lee and what sadness his deeds had wrought upon someone else whom he did not know. But for the most part he felt young and strong and was not guilty for feeling so.

He was breathing, and they were not.

His legs carried him swiftly over the decay that was hidden in the ground and though they might take flight in heaven, they would never step lightly over the wet grass and feel how wonderful the night could be when a cool breeze came along, as one was doing now. He felt alive.

All this changed five plots in to the right.

There, written in stone, was an affirmation of the one thing that, for three days, he had been all about.

HERE LIES JOE, BELOVED HUSBAND OF CANDACE. TRUE LOVE WILL NEVER DIE.

A strong breeze blew through the graveyard and then left, taking Candace, who was wandering off and reading headstones, with it.

He dropped to his knees on the thick carpet of grass of Just Plain Joe's grave and his palm swept over the wet blades and he knew that although his journey was over, it would never really end.

There wasn't a man alive could compete with Joe.

No, not while alive.

Guns and bats and prayers to Jesus were worthless and if he could have struck a deal with the Devil, he would have. To trade places with Joe, with that lucky bastard, for just five minutes. To lie in the dirt and be shrouded in the smell of innocence and naïveté. Of faith and belief and of an unwavering adoration.

To go cleanly and quietly while still young, and in love.

To be missed like that was surely worth a few years of despair on God's green earth.

He wept, not openly, but silently. The tears he shed, inside of himself, would never escape and would never dry and they would never satisfy his pain like the tears of a mourner. They would be with him always, behind his eyes and in his heart, inside his soul, where they would submerge him in misery when awake and torment him with nightmares when asleep.

He wiped the beaded rain from the headstone so that he could read again the words there, and then he sat on that hallowed ground, leaning one shoulder against the stone marker, and rested for a few moments now that he had come to the end of his journey.

There was no grand reward for what he had done. There was no end to justify his means, there were just two murders on his hands, and in his heart, and at that moment, there was nothing else to him at all.

Candace crept up behind him and laid her palm on the back of his neck and the brief sensation of her skin upon his touched off an explosion that started at the base of his neck and consumed all of his brain in just a matter of seconds.

Still grasping the tire iron, he sprang to his feet and swung blindly at Joe's tombstone. He felt a pain in his hands upon impact that ignited the nerves in his arms and shoulders and spread between his

Collecting Candace

shoulder blades like a warm river of blood. He struck again, sending chips of granite flying into his eyes and his face. One big piece hit him just above his right eyebrow. It cut deep and the blood flowed down over the bridge of his nose and the corner of his mouth. Candace screamed and covered her head. She moved away to the next row and took refuge behind Our Lord but it was no good. His betrayal exploded all over the cemetery until she too got soaked with rain and stone.

The rain started to come down hard and some got into his eyes, mixing with the blood on his face and his tears and smearing him in the stuff. He stumbled back, doubled over with pain and choking on his own breaths and he swung again, this time missing the tombstone entirely and propelling the crowbar from his slippery grasp and sending it crashing against an old tree, where it cut a gash of bark out and then fell to the ground with a thud.

The top layer of earth was soaked, but just beneath, where his boot slipped and left a wide track, it was still dry as a bone and dusty too. There wasn't anything as dramatic as a bolt of lightning and Jesus did not speak to him from heaven on high, there was only the soft patter of rainwater hitting the tops of grave stones and the sound of the dog rustling around in the thick bushes, looking for cover or maybe a raccoon.

He had nothing to lose. He never did have anything to lose, and this he would have known from the very first night if she'd brought him here before she took him anywhere. If she'd told him. If he'd known. It was never clear to her, his plan and his reasons but there was someone else who knew exactly where this was all headed, right from the beginning.

He'd been sucker-punched by Our Heavenly Father

wanted for questioning in a couple of murders

and sure the angels were there too,

beloved husband of Candace

to grab him by the balls and drag him kicking and screaming to hell

till death do us part

only after laying his eyes upon such a sight as he'd seen in this graveyard tonight he went willingly for sure

cuff him, watch his head

'cause there was no place left to go.

He spun around on his heel and lunged for Candace, whose body was now pressed against the wet concrete likeness of the Blessed Virgin Mary.

The sight of this was more that enough to touch him off.

His wet hands were on her all at once, touching her, feeling her, molding themselves to the contour of her shoulders and then further down, to her breasts. He grasped the white folds of fabric and tore the thin gauze down the middle, exposing her torso and the wet flesh there, just like he'd seen it that first morning when she came out of the shower.

Dropping to his knees, he slid his hands down her sides till they came to rest on her hips, there he grasped her tightly and pulled her in as he pressed his ear to her wet stomach. The rain was all over them, the mud too, for now the ground was wet at least a quarter of an inch down. She cried and

Collecting Candace

writhed in his arms and her fingers tore at his hair, she sobbed for loving him so and for being so frightened. Candace did not understand the consequences of Joe's death, not then, not now.

As far as Candace was concerned, everlasting love had nothing to do with heaven or Mary or tombstone sayings. It was about need. It was about destroying the motel room when she was not there. It was about killing a man

for Chrissakes

with her right out there in the hallway and not expecting to get laid or anything afterward.

Mostly it was about sticking around, but it certainly was not about family plots or about turning water into wine.

This she told him, crying and choking on rainwater, she begged him to stop and to stand up and go with her. To go home. To be her husband. She begged him to just love her and forget all that shit of the past and why in the world would he want to visit a graveyard on his wedding night anyway?

But he could only cry. That, and hold on tighter.

He pulled her down with him and they wrestled in the fresh mud, it splattering their faces like blood does, all thin and watered down it got in their mouths and they spit it out but they still tasted it on one another's lips. Dirt. Grass. Salt.

The rain was practically not there at all but it felt like a hurricane in that graveyard.

His hands slid over her body, just like he'd imagined they did that night in the motel. His fingers took refuge there in the small of her back where he touched her softness and kneaded her flesh between his fingers. He smoothed down the matted hairs there, those little blond hairs that swayed like wheat, and then he lifted himself off the ground and turned her over and bent to kiss them.

A stronger love he never did feel.

His tongue was hot from fever and from rage, he licked her down and between gasps she choked out more dirt and begged him no please not here and said I can't but he could not hear her anymore.

it seems there was this murder

He pushed what was left of her wedding gown up over her thighs and hips with his nose, nuzzling her moist flesh along the way and tasting parts of her that, till tonight, he had only dreamed of.

They rolled together and the mud splashed in his eye but he kept going. He hooked his fingers into her panties and yanked them down and he felt this heat

we have witnesses

that Gainesville would never be able to match

that can place you in the general vicinity

and with one free hand he fumbled with his jeans.

On his knees, before Mary, Mother of God, he meant to take his bride. He thrust forward and she cried out his name and he came to her. Her fingernails dug into his forearms and he felt her close down around him all at once and Jesus fucking Christ if he didn't believe in Heaven at precisely that moment.

It was wet. That, he noticed first—the rain, his sweat, his body, and hers. The chill was gone and it was only warm and moist and it was what he had been waiting to feel all this time, for as long as he could remember.

Collecting Candace

The next thing he felt was the pain of slamming his forehead into a slab of white marble. Blood stained Mary's feet and it gushed from his fresh wound and he closed one eye to keep it from getting in but his body shuddered and his muscles went weak

true love will never die

and he bit his lip to keep himself awake but there was no need 'cause she was biting him now

I killed a man I stole a dog

and he experienced nothing but the light

Candace I need you

and then he passed out.

the end

He awoke, bloodied, sore and wet, with no sign of Candace, and with the toe of somebody's cowboy boot nudging the tip of his nose and pushing his face back and forth in the mud.

"You alive, son?"

He heard the voice from above

take me St. Peter

and for a minute he thought well goddamnit she was right but when he opened one eye he saw only a tall figure, silhouetted by the sun behind, and the flash of mirrored sunglasses reflecting his own ratty figure back at him. He shut it again.

It was hot, Lord, it was humid too. Felt like the fucking Amazon jungle or something. Didn't feel like Florida. Didn't feel like anything he'd ever known before.

hell

He groaned at having found himself alive.

"I think he's alive..."

"Any sign of the girl?"

"None. There's some blood on 'im though. Hey. Hey, you."

He felt the boot again and he could smell the leather. It was old and worn and smelled like an old horse blanket. The silver-capped tip came into his nose again. Cold and hard, it awoke him rudely this time and he groaned even more loudly but did not move. Whoever's shoe that was moved it back out of the way, four or five inches from his face, where the toe smeared over the grass softly like it was trying to wipe itself clean.

He tried to open the other eye but it was caked with blood and his eyelashes were matted in mud. He struggled to sit up, he leaned back against the Blessed Virgin Mary and tried to wipe his face, but his arm too was covered in sludge and wet grass and it only made a bigger mess.

From above, a hand offered a clean white handkerchief and he took it.

He spit into the cloth and then held it tenderly over his eyelid but his skull was so badly bruised that it sent a searing pain through his brain and the rest of his body. There were fat drops of rain resting like Jell-O on the tombstone. He dabbed the already-stained handkerchief into the water and held it to his face again and this time it worked. Working the wound gingerly, moving in small circles, he wiped away most of the crud. He opened the other eye and saw now two tall figures over him, standing in the narrow path between the grave he sat on and the one next to it. He could not make out their faces but he needn't anyway. He didn't have to see the color of their fucking eyes to know they were not angels.

Candace lied.

Bracing himself against the headstone, he extended his legs, ignoring the pop of his knees, and pushed his boot heels along the ground, trying to get some friction and get himself upright, but his feet just slid in the soaked grass and made wide, deep tracks. He gave up after only one try and rested again on the grave marker.

"There's a dog here."

"Hey, hey you..." the voice from above spoke softly in his direction. "That your dog? What's its name?"

He ignored the question and instead only concentrated on cleaning up the excess shit that seemed to be covering him from head to toe. The handkerchief, which was now muddied and soaked with blood, did more harm than good but still he wiped it over his face and over the backs of his hands. Mud, thick and cold like day-old mashed potatoes, clung to his bare skin just inside the waistband of his jeans. It covered his arms too and was caked so badly between his fingers that he had to scoop it out with his thumb and fling it to the ground.

The sun was coming up right over a white marble angel, and the light bounced along its head and shoulders and shone down in his eyes.

come into the light

No, he wasn't gonna fall for that a second time. He smiled sarcastically.

Pretty fucking tricky, this one is

"There's a ball bat here in the car. It's looking pretty bad. Come see."

He peered out as the pair of boots that had woken him were turned on their heels and walked twenty-five, maybe thirty feet to the north and stood there beside the Maverick's front tire where they shifted back and forth in the gravel. It had seemed so far last night, it had seemed like they'd walked for miles and miles to reach this one plot. Now, even with his blurred vision and confused perspective, he could see that it was hardly spitting distance from there to the car.

Three or four other voices came from over near the Maverick but they sounded so much alike it was hard to say exactly. The police radio crackled in the still morning; its rude, staccato tone irritated him more than the boot in the nose did.

He watched, low to the ground, as the boots made their way back for him, trudging this time right over the soft mounds and not even trying to stay on the pathways.

"Party's over, son, let's get going." An arm came down and he took it, wrapping his fingers around the forearm as tightly as he could and it lifted him off the ground. His body, aching with soreness and tired from the journey, sagged when he stood. His shoulders drooped and his head was cocked to one side, on account of he only had one good eye this morning.

He stood eye-level with the uniform standing before him. There was a clinking sound as something was produced from a back pocket. He turned around obligingly and lifted his arms, wrists together, six or seven inches from his ass. The steel bracelets fit into place a little tightly and then his arms dropped again.

"You're armed and dangerous, did you know that?"

He did not respond. He only lifted his head and looked out past the back fence of the graveyard, wondering where Candace had gotten to.

"Least, that's what they say. Armed and dangerous." The voice snorted but not sarcastically. It was
more the way that Candace said 'Cause it was dead.

He smiled at remembering that moment and
then he turned to face the other two uniforms that
were approaching. They escorted him over the dead,
where he had felt so alive and so superior last night.
This morning, he was humbled.

They trudged over a husband and wife and he
looked back longingly.

Did she lie?

"You're pretty beat up, son. We'd better get
someone to look at that eye."

The Maverick sat just where it had been parked
last night. Now its doors, hood, and trunk were
open wide and all their belongings had been spilled
out onto the dewy overgrown weeds where they were
getting all mixed up together. The ball bat. The gun,
no bullets. Coke cans, candy wrappers. A wine bottle, empty. A plastic bag full of clothes soaked in
Danny Ray's blood. His eyes searched the rubble for
the Bowie knife but then remembered it was one of
the things that had been left behind. With little effort, his forefinger dug into his back pocket and the
folded up construction paper card was tossed onto
the ground to join the other crap he had brought
along. Some glitter sea spray trickled to the ground
where it caught the light just right, and sparkled in
his eyes.

He was yanked back to the right, where a police
car sat with its rear door open wide.

"Watch his head."

Collecting Candace

The dog went with Animal Control, and so he was left alone with himself, God, and two lawmen who sat in the front seat and looked at him with curiosity and amazement.

"Boy, you've been having yourself a hell of a time, haven't you?"

They read his rights and his head buzzed from all that wine he'd drunk the night before.

I love you truly.

He worried again about the Missus.

The police car rocked gently from side to side, clumsily finding its path over the dirt road leading out of the cemetery. They passed Rev. Bob's house, and soon were back on the main road that would lead to town, and then finally to the station house.

There were no particular thoughts that filled his head as he found himself being escorted to justice. It was not like the night in the motel when he bargained for his soul. This morning, he had nothing in particular to say to God. It was Candace who got that bright idea in the first place. And with her gone, there was no sense in keeping up appearances.

He was not revengeful, as Candace had put it. He was not mad at her and he only loved her that much more. On a more practical note, he did wish he hadn't lost consciousness so soon last night.

His thoughts naturally went back to the Hi-N-Dri where he first met her and where all of this first occurred to him. And to The Box, back at the house, still full of his father's shit.

He thought of his closet back home, his clothes all pushed to the right to make room for whomever. Whatever. It didn't matter no more.

The police car pulled onto the main road and kicked up a cloud of dry, Florida dust as it picked up speed and headed for its destination. His body ached. He itched all over. He shook his head like wet dog and some matted, greasy hair slapped him in the eye and then one tiny piece of uncooked rice fell onto his lap. He wanted to pick it up but, with his hands cuffed behind his back, he could only stare at it there, resting delicately on his thigh.

They sped up and the cops laughed back and forth about all kinds of shit and they teased him good-naturedly and blipped the siren for fun. Both of them missed the lone figure standing on the side of the road, facing away from traffic and cradling a beat-up piece of plastic in her hands.

But he did not.

He watched her out the back of the window, watched her in the bright, hot sunlight

Christ, gonna be a scorcher

watched her getting smaller and smaller till all he could see was the brown horizon where she was standing a moment ago.

There was nothing but the heat, the dust, and a brand new day.

And there stood Candace. 0 for 4.